SARAH MLYNOWSKI

Illustrations by Maxine Vee

Scholastic Press

New York

Library of Congress Cataloging-in-Publication Data available

ISBN 978-1-338-62825-8

10 9 8 7 6 5 4 3 2 1   22 23 24 25 26

Printed in the U.S.A.   37

First edition, September 2022

Book design by Abby Dening and Elizabeth B. Parisi

For my daughter Anabelle Swidler,
who insisted that her bedtime story
should really be a book

✳

* 1 *

How It Started

Dear Addie,

I'm not sure I should be writing this.

But it feels like the right thing to do. Even if I don't know much about you besides your name.

Addie.

Is that short for something? Addison? Adeline? Adam? Addacadabra?

Anyway, hi, Addie. I'm Becca. Nice to meet you.

When you read this, please don't pass it around to all your friends while you laugh at how weird I am. Please? Good. Thank you.

Now, where should I start?

I guess when I got the magic box in the mail. That's when everything went bananas. Or maybe when I made the wish? OMG, wait until I tell you about the scary blond woman!

Deep breath. I'm getting ahead of myself. You need to know *why* I made the wish in the first place. So let me start with what happened a week ago. Last Monday.

I was standing outside my brick elementary school with my (then) best friend, Harper Mehta. We live and go to school on the Upper West Side, which is a neighborhood in New York City.

The students always line up in the schoolyard before the first bell rings. That day, it was sunny and warm out, even though it was already October. All around us I could hear the sounds of the city: taxicabs honking, buses pulling up, people hurrying to the subway.

"Are you ready," I said to Harper, "to hear the plan for my birthday sleepover on Saturday?"

I was excited. Very excited. Harper always slept over on my birthday, and we always had the best time.

"Mm-hmm," Harper said, but she was looking at her phone.

"I bought white T-shirts, scrunchies, pillowcases, *and* pencil cases," I said. "And, of course, every tie-dye color. Blue, red, green, yellow, purple, pink . . ."

Harper glanced up. "That sounds like a lot for just the two of us."

"There is no such thing as too much tie-dye," I said. I was wearing a tie-dyed sweatshirt right then. Harper and I had made matching ones over the summer. "And we'll have cake, and stay up late, and do story-a-thon!" I smiled. Story-a-thon is when Harper and I each make up one sentence of a story until we get to the end. That was our favorite hangout activity.

Principal Bort was letting kids into the building super slowly. Harper and I stepped forward in the line.

"Well, um, about your birthday . . ." Harper began, and my shoulders clenched.

"What?" I asked.

"I can't sleep over," she said quickly. "I have to get up early on Sunday morning for a chess tournament."

My heart sank. "Oh. Okay. You can't skip it?"

"No," Harper said. "But I'll still come over on Saturday for cake and stuff."

I felt queasy.

Harper and I met in kindergarten, when our moms arranged a playdate for us. Harper's mom dropped her off at my apartment, and at first we just stared at each other, blinking awkwardly. Then my mom suggested that we play Legos. Harper and I built a Lego castle, and soon we invented a game we called Dragons & Wizards. From that day on, we were best friends. And for the next four years, we were in the same class. Until this year. Fifth grade. I was put in 5A, and Harper was put in 5B.

Imagine the sound I made when Principal Bort read out the class lists on the first day of school. I sounded like a bleating goat. Not that I've met many goats, since New York City doesn't really have farms. I'm a little scared of goats, actually. And sheep. And birds. And most animals. But anyway. I made a strange sound. Because not being in Harper's class was very upsetting.

I couldn't believe that Harper wasn't going to sleep over on my birthday. I tried to take deep breaths to calm down.

"Well, can you come over after school today?" I asked.

But she didn't answer. She was waving excitedly to someone across the yard.

That someone was Georgette Dimopoulus, the purple-haired chess champion of the fifth grade.

Who was also a champion friend hogger.

Georgette is in 5B with Harper. One day Harper invited Georgette to play Dragons & Wizards with us at lunch, but after fifteen minutes, Georgette had convinced Harper that the game was babyish, and that we should play Two Square instead. So I agreed, whatever, but it's Two Square, not Three Square, so one of us always sat out. It's not the world's best game for three people, now is it?

Georgette also convinced Harper to sign up for after-school chess. So then it was chess this, chess that, blah blah blah. Sometimes I imagined snapping all the tiny chess pieces in half, if you want to know the truth.

Georgette pushed into line behind us.

"Go on Friendstagram right now," she told Harper. "Remember the kid who cried at the chess tournament last week? Someone posted a video of him sobbing!" She blew a bubble with her pink gum.

Harper's eyes widened into saucers, and she began tapping at her phone screen. "No! Way! So embarrassing!"

5

"Such a crybaby."

Ouch. Georgette isn't the nicest. Also, she and Harper are obsessed with Friendstagram, this app that I wasn't allowed to be on. I wasn't even allowed to have a phone. It was one of my mom's billion rules.

Harper and Georgette were giggling at the video when we reached the school doors.

Principal Bort shook his head at us. He's bald and has piercing dark eyes.

"Miss Singer," he told me. "Your shoelaces are untied."

"Sorry, Mr. Bort," I said. I knelt down to retie my sneakers.

"Miss Mehta. Phone away. Immediately."

"Sorry, Mr. Bort," Harper said, stuffing her phone in her bag.

"Miss Dimopoulus. Get rid of your gum."

He is a man of few words. But they are always harsh words.

While Georgette ran to the garbage can to throw out her gum, I walked into school with Harper.

"So can you?" I asked her. "Come over today?"

"I . . . I can't," she said, hesitating. "I'm going to Georgette's."

Did she invite me to go to Georgette's, too? No, she

did not. I guess that was fair since Georgette and I weren't exactly friends—we were just friends through Harper. We were friends-in-law. And I hadn't invited Georgette to my birthday sleepover. I didn't want to talk about Friendstagram and chess the whole time. My mom had said I could invite some of the other kids in my class. But I don't like big parties, and well, I wasn't really friends with anyone else besides Harper.

"I'll see you at lunch, though?" I asked her.

"Sure," Harper said. Georgette came inside, and the two of them hurried up the stairs. I trailed behind, trying not to show how let down I felt.

When we reached the fifth-floor hallway, I watched Harper and Georgette disappear into the 5B classroom. I paused outside the 5A classroom door, my throat tight.

"Becca, are you going to come inside or *block* the door the *whole* time?"

My teacher, Ms. Michaels, was watching me from inside the classroom, her hands on her hips. She always wears thick winged black eyeliner. She also likes to emphasize every few words dramatically, like she's starring in a play.

"Sorry," I said, but it ended up coming out as another bleating goat sound.

I went inside and took my seat in the last row of the class, next to Shep Harris.

Shep has shaggy brown hair and wears sweatpants and his school gym sweatshirt every day. He was bent over a notebook, drawing, as usual.

Elijah Weinberg sat on the other side of me. He was busy talking to his two best friends, Emma Ono and Elizabeth King, who sat right in front of us. Elijah, Emma, and Elizabeth call themselves the Three Es. They make up dances together at lunch and wear a lot of accessories. Rubber bracelets. Long necklaces. Rings. Sparkly barrettes. Colorful scarves. They always seemed to have a lot of fun, but I'd never hung out with them.

"Let's get to work, everyone!" Ms. Michaels said. "We have a *big* week—spelling quiz on *Wednesday* and math test on *Friday*, right after the *assembly*."

There was an excited murmur around the classroom. The Friday assembly is when they announce the Super Student of the Week. That honor usually goes to someone who's aced a test or won a chess tournament. Yes, Georgette has been Super Student. Twice. It's never been me. I am not really a student-of-the-week kind of kid.

"Willow," Ms. Michaels said to a girl in the front row,

"*please* put your book away and collect *everyone's* math homework."

I reached into my bag to get my multiplication worksheet, which I had done the night before.

Hmm. Where was it? I looked in the big pocket. I looked in the small pocket. I looked in the super-small pocket, which featured an impressive collection of gum wrappers and broken pencils.

The worksheet wasn't there. I must have forgotten it at home. See? Not really a student of the week.

Shoot, I thought as Willow approached my row.

Shep handed her his assignment. Then Willow turned to me. Her dark brown hair was in a loose bun on her head, and she was wearing a white sweatshirt that said *One More Chapter* in green. Her earrings were pizza slices.

"I can't find it," I whispered to her. This was bad. Really bad. Ms. Michaels is not exactly understanding about missed homework.

Willow grimaced. "Oh no."

"Yeah," I agreed. I slowly, sadly raised my hand.

"Becca?" Ms. Michaels said.

"Um, I'm so, so, so sorry, but I think I forgot my assignment at home," I said. "Can I bring it tomorrow?"

The room went silent.

"You *think* you forgot it, or you *did* forget it?" Ms. Michaels's winged eyes narrowed.

"I did forget it," I mumbled. I wished I could shrink and hide in my pencil case.

My teacher frowned. "I see. That seems very *careless*. And you expect me to let you bring it in *tomorrow*? Would that be *fair* to the other kids in the class?"

"Probably not. I'm sorry." I hung my head.

"I'm *disappointed* in you, Becca," Ms. Michaels added.

I felt my face flush. And my arms. Oh no. I knew what that meant.

I touched my cheek and felt a hive forming. My skin is really sensitive—and when I get stressed, I sometimes get a stress rash, or hives, which look like little mosquito bites. They're itchy and hot and very embarrassing.

Deep breaths. Deep breaths.

I tried to calm myself down. That's what my doctor told me to do.

I just had to make it to lunch. Harper would make me feel better.

Ms. Michaels turned back to the whiteboard, and I sank into my seat, trying to disappear.

When it was finally time to eat, I grabbed my lunch bag and ran to the cafeteria.

Harper and Georgette were sitting together, eating grilled cheese sandwiches and french fries from the cafeteria. Yum. Mom had packed me tofu and broccoli. Yawn.

I sat down next to Harper.

"So I forgot my math homework—" I began.

"Shhh," Georgette interrupted me, dipping her french fry in ketchup. "I'm explaining a chess move."

"Oh. Sorry."

Georgette and Harper chattered on about thunderbolts and endgame sacrifices while I quietly ate my tofu and broccoli.

"What happened to your neck?" Georgette asked, finally acknowledging me. "Do you have chicken pox or something?" She scooted away from me.

"No," I said quickly. "It's just . . ."

"She gets this weird rash," Harper said.

I felt myself blush. It *is* a weird rash. I know it's weird. But did Harper have to call it weird in front of Georgette?

"But it's not contagious or anything," Harper added.

"Maybe you shouldn't sit so close to us," Georgette said, wrinkling her nose. "Just in case."

"Yeah, of course," I said, my cheeks heating up even more.

I shifted over slightly and waited until Georgette and Harper were done eating and we could go outside. Once out the door, Georgette ran up ahead, but I put my hand on Harper's arm to get her to wait a sec. I motioned her over to the area between the brick wall and where the Three Es were learning some sort of intricate dance that involved a lot of hand movements.

"Can we talk? Just us?" I asked Harper.

"But Georgette is waiting," Harper said, fidgeting.

"I know, but I . . . well, I didn't love that you called my rash weird."

She blinked. "You call it weird all the time."

"But that's different from you calling it weird in front of Georgette," I said, feeling a lump in my throat.

"I'm sorry. I shouldn't have said that. Can we go find her now?" Harper asked, glancing longingly toward Georgette.

"But I haven't talked to you all day," I said.

"We talked this morning," she said.

"I talked, you played on your phone," I muttered.

She narrowed her eyes. "Excuse me?"

And then the words rushed out of me like vomit. "I just . . . Georgette gets you all day and I barely get to see you and I want to complain about Ms. Michaels! Can't we hang out just the two of us? Please? You're supposed to be my best friend, but lately you're not acting like it."

Harper glanced down at her hands. "Becca . . . look . . . this is hard to say."

My heart started to beat a million miles a minute, like I was running in gym class. "What? What's hard to say?"

And then she said it. I can't even write it, Addie.

I have to write it.

Here it comes.

She said: "I don't think I want to be best friends anymore."

There was silence. Time slowed down. A ball went whizzing by my head.

"You don't *think*?" I croaked out. "Or you *don't*?"

"I don't," she rushed to say, biting her thumbnail. "I'm sorry if this hurts your feelings, I really am. But since we started fifth grade, I just don't consider you my best friend, and I want to be honest about that. We're different than we used to be. We're interested in different things. I like Friendstagram and chess and Two Square and plants—"

Plants? This was the first I'd heard about plants.

"—and I'm kind of over tie-dye and story-a-thon."

My heart sank. "We don't have to do tie-dye. Or story-a-thon."

"You're missing the point. We're just not into the same things anymore. And it's okay if we go different ways. My mom says it's part of growing up."

I didn't know what to say. "But . . ." My voice trailed off. "But I'm not allowed on Friendstagram! I would be into it if I was allowed!"

"Still," Harper said. She picked at her thumbnail. "We can be friends. Just not *best* friends." Across the playground, Georgette was waving at us. At Harper.

"Are you going to be best friends with someone else?" I asked.

"Probably," she said slowly.

"With Georgette?" I asked.

"Yeah."

"How could you choose Georgette over me? She's not even nice! She bosses us around!" I could hear my voice rising. I hardly ever got mad at Harper, but I was starting to panic.

Harper crossed her arms. "She does not."

"She won't let us play Dragons & Wizards anymore! She makes you go to chess tournaments!"

"She doesn't *make* me do anything. I like spending time with her."

"I can't believe you would choose her over me!" I yelled.

I realized that despite the dancing and chatting and balls whizzing around us, it seemed like everyone in the yard had stopped what they were doing and were watching me and Harper.

Don't cry. Don't cry. Don't cry.

"I'm sorry," Harper said softly.

"But what about my birthday?" I asked.

"I can still come," she said.

I imagined how uncomfortable I'd be the whole time, knowing she didn't want to be there. Knowing she'd rather be playing chess or Two Square with Georgette. Or watering plants.

"Never mind," I said, my heart breaking. "I don't want to spend my birthday with you anymore. I don't even know how I can be *regular* friends with you anymore."

Harper opened her mouth, closed it, and then spoke. "Fine. If you don't want to be friends, then we won't be friends. I'm going to find Georgette now. Bye."

Bye? BYE? I couldn't believe it. Did my best friend of five years just end our best friendship by saying BYE? IN THE SCHOOLYARD? Really?!

The truth hit me in the face like freezing cold water: My best friend had dumped me. And I had no other friends.

* 2 *

The Box

My eyes filled with tears. What was I supposed to do? Chase Harper through the schoolyard? Tell her no? You can't say no to someone dumping you, can you?

I watched Harper reach Georgette. They glanced at me. Harper shook her head. Georgette laughed.

I turned and ran back inside, through the cafeteria, past the library, and into the single bathroom, which was thankfully empty. I slammed the door shut and turned the metal lock. Then I stared at my now-very-hivey neck, face, and arms in the mirror. I tried to calm myself by taking deep breaths, which is not something you really want to do in a smelly bathroom.

I leaned against the cool white tiles and let the tears spill down my cheeks.

When the bell rang, I wiped my eyes with the back of my hand. I had to get to class.

I went to turn the lock. It didn't budge. I tried again. It still wouldn't budge.

The door was jammed. I heard kids' voices and laughter out in the hall.

"Hello?" I called out, starting to panic. "I'm stuck! Can someone help me? Anyone?" I pounded on the door. "Anyone?"

There was no answer. No one could hear me.

I sank to the cold floor and started to sob.

"Worst day ever," I muttered.

There was a gust of air from one of the vents and the overhead lights flickered off.

Great. Not only was I a friendless, hivey crybaby, I was now also trapped in a pitch-black bathroom.

Then the lights came back on. At least I had that.

After school, my mom was waiting for me in the pickup area. Since we live so close by, Mom walks me to and from school every day.

As soon as she saw me, she put her arms around me and hugged me close. She smelled like Play-Dough.

"Are you okay?" she asked.

"No," I said.

Mom is the director of a preschool in our neighborhood. She was wearing a black blazer, black pants, a white button-down shirt, and pearl earrings. Everyone says we look alike. We have the same pale skin and curly dark blond hair. But I wear mine long and Mom's hair is short. And she doesn't get red blotches all over her face.

"The nurse called me about your hives. I said it was all right to give you an antihistamine." My mom pulled back and studied my cheeks. "What happened?"

"I accidentally locked myself in the bathroom. For forty-five minutes," I told her. My stress hives had gotten much, much worse in those forty-five minutes.

"Oh no!"

"Oh yes. Some third grader finally heard my yells and found Principal Bort, who got me out with the help of three teachers and the janitor. Principal Bort sent me to the nurse when he saw the hives."

Thank goodness the nurse didn't make me return to class. I waited in his office for the final bell to ring and for kids to clear out before heading to my classroom to get my backpack. That way I didn't have to see anyone.

"I'm so sorry, hon," Mom said as we walked down 90th Street. "It's terrible that you were stuck in the bathroom."

"That wasn't even what caused the hives," I said. I blinked back tears. "First, I forgot my homework. And then Harper told me she didn't want to be friends anymore."

My mom stopped on the corner. "She told you that?"

"Yes. And she's not coming to my birthday."

Mom winced. "What? I'm going to text her mother."

"No, Mom, you can't. Promise you won't. Promise. That would make everything worse."

She sighed. "Do you have other friends you want to invite? Maybe some of the kids from your new class?"

"I don't even talk to them. I barely know them."

"That's how you *get* to know them," Mom said.

"I'll think about it," I said, even though I knew I wouldn't. Besides, it was already Monday. How could I make friends in time to invite them to a Saturday party? Impossible.

Mom and I crossed Broadway, and we walked past the Pilates studio, Goodwill store, Starbucks, and a nail salon called Oasis. I had never been inside Oasis. My mother gets a manicure once a month, but she says it's absurd for a kid to get one.

"What about your friend from the second floor?" Mom asked as we turned onto our street. "You could invite her to your birthday!"

"What? Who?"

"You know, the girl who plays the sax," she said excitedly.

"Mom, she's six. I don't want to celebrate my birthday with a six-year-old."

"What about Rose, then?"

"My old babysitter? No! Mom! Come on. I don't even want a party. We'll just forget my birthday this year."

"Don't worry," Mom said, putting her arm around me. "I bet Harper will come around."

I swallowed hard. I didn't see that happening.

We stopped outside the blue awning of our apartment building.

"You go on in," Mom said. "Your brother is already home. I just need to run over to the Kosher Marketplace to pick up dinner."

We're Jewish, and although we're not very religious, we try to keep kosher. That means we don't eat meat and dairy together, and we never eat pork or shellfish.

The Kosher Marketplace has some great stuff—potato pancakes, raisin noodle kugel, crispy chicken schnitzel. But my mom is very into health food. Dinner is usually baked chicken or salmon with steamed veggies and brown rice.

"Any chance we could get a pizza tonight?" I asked hopefully. "That would cheer me up." There are tons of pizza places on the Upper West Side. (My family eats from non-kosher restaurants; we just don't order non-kosher items—so no pepperoni on our pizza.)

"Pizza isn't very nutritious," Mom said.

Of course. My mom's rules include but are not limited to: No pizza except on rare occasions. No junk food. Lights-out at eight for me, ten for my older brother, Brahm. No TV or video games during the week.

She unlocked the front door of our building to let me in. "Be sure to get started on your homework," she told me. "I don't want you forgetting it again."

I flinched. I knew Mom wouldn't let that slide. "'Kay. See you soon."

I walked into our small lobby, where our super, Mr. Wangins, was mopping the floor. His parrot, Doodles, was perched on his shoulder. Doodles is bright blue, and when she's not hanging out with Mr. Wangins, she likes to fly around our building's back courtyard.

Oh, and Doodles hates me. I'm not kidding.

"Ahoy, Becca, how's your day?" Mr. Wangins asked cheerfully. Mr. Wangins has been the super of our building for twenty years. He lives in an apartment on the first floor and takes care of everything: repairs, packages, recycling. He's very friendly. Unlike Doodles.

"Go away!" Doodles squawked at me.

See?

"Stop it, Doodles," Mr. Wangins said. "Be nice to Becca!"

"My day was fine," I lied, heading for the elevator. I was eager to get upstairs.

"Oh, Becca! You got a package in the mail," Mr. Wangins said.

I turned around. "I did?"

"Yup. I left it in the mailroom."

"Oh! Thank you," I said.

"Go away!" Doodles squawked as I hurried into the mailroom.

There, in the corner with the other packages, was a box. A square cardboard box, about the size of a small toaster. It was covered in cute stickers.

And it was addressed to . . .

Me.

Me?

Yes. Me.

I never get packages! But in cursive black writing, on the top of the box, it read:

Becca Singer
416 West 91st Street, Apt 7G
New York, New York 10027

There was no return address, but there was a big black sparkly stamp in the top right corner that said *Forever*.

Maybe it was from my dad?

My parents got divorced when I was four. My dad used to live in Brooklyn, and Brahm and I stayed with him every other weekend. But when Dad got laid off last year, he had to move to Santa Monica, California, for a new tech job. This was the first time I wouldn't be seeing Dad on my birthday. It felt kind of sad.

It felt really sad, actually.

I picked up the box. It wasn't heavy. I shook it a little, and something rattled inside.

Intrigued, I carried the box over to the elevator, pulled open the collapsible metal door, and stepped inside. Our elevator is super slow. When it finally reached the seventh floor, I got out and unlocked the door to my apartment.

We live in a classic six, which means our apartment has two bedrooms, a kitchen, a dining room, a living room, and what used to be a maid's room, which is now our storage and laundry room. My mom has the big bedroom, my brother has the second bedroom, so I live in the dining room, although it's not really a dining room because it has a door on it and everything. My mom loves the apartment because it's prewar, which means it was built before World War II and it's pretty old. It also means the ceilings are high and the floors are wood.

I dropped my backpack on the floor and kicked off my sneakers but held on to the box.

Brahm, my twelve-year-old brother, was pacing around

the living room, earbuds in his ears, repeating words in Hebrew. He was practicing for his bar mitzvah. It's this December, when he turns thirteen.

I go to Hebrew school on Thursday afternoons. But I won't start studying for my bat mitzvah for another couple of years since I'm only nine turning ten. I'm one of the younger kids in my grade, because my birthday is close to the end of the year. And before you ask, no, I don't have any friends in Hebrew school, either: I somehow ended up in a class of all seven- and eight-year-olds.

Anyway. My brother's inviting over fifty friends to his bar mitzvah party.

I wouldn't have one friend to invite, never mind fifty.

"Mom's getting dinner," I told Brahm.

He gave me a bug-eyed look.

"Mom's getting dinner!" I said again.

He sighed. Turned off his audio. "What?"

"Mom's getting dinner. I asked for pizza, but she said no. Surprise."

He glared at me. "I don't care. And I was doing something and now I have to start over."

He turned his audio back on and walked away from me, his usual unpleasant self.

I rolled my eyes. Brahm didn't talk to his friends the

way he talked to me—obviously. If he did, he wouldn't have any.

I carried the package into my room, closing the door behind me. I like my dining room/bedroom. Mom painted the walls lavender, my favorite color. I keep everything neat, too. I like my stuff organized. Although you do not want to look under my bed.

"Hi, Twinkle," I said to my betta fish, who was swimming around in his fishbowl on my dresser. Twinkle is over four years old, which might be a world record for a betta fish. The last few fish we had lasted two months, max.

I say "we," but Twinkle is really mine. I picked him out, I feed him, and I clean his bowl.

I gently set the box on my desk, next to my laptop. On top of my laptop was my forgotten math homework. Awesome.

I eyed the box. Maybe Dad had gotten me a phone? That would make up for the crummy day I'd had.

I hesitated before opening the box. Sometimes the promise of something is better than the real thing, you know?

The lid was taped closed with clear packing tape. I took out my scissors to carefully open it and then flipped the top up.

The interior of the box was decorated with tiny circles. And sitting in the center of the box was an emerald-green glittery pouch. Ooh.

I took out the pouch and opened it carefully. Inside was a delicate bracelet made of turquoise and gold beads of different sizes.

It was beautiful.

There was also a letter in the box on a sheet of old-looking paper.

The words were written in black cursive that matched the handwriting on the box. Tingles spread up my arms as I started to read.

★ 3 ★

The Bracelet

Because you're blue,
This bracelet is now for you.
Speak one wish to make it true.
(There are some things it cannot do.)
Keep the box to mail the magic off
When you are through.
Take care and beware.
Hugs and kisses,
And best wishes.

I blinked. *What?*

This was from my dad?

Best wishes did sound like something a grown-up would

say at the end of a letter. Like *Kind regards* or *Sincerely yours*. But my dad wouldn't write a mysterious poem.

Was it from someone else?

My dad's parents aren't alive anymore. My mom's parents, Bubby and Zadie, live on Long Island, and they had given me a gift certificate for my birthday when I saw them two weeks ago.

I stared down at the bracelet in my hand. Then I reread the note.

Why did it say *Take care and beware*? Beware of what?

And why did the note look like it was a hundred years old?

The bracelet and the pouch looked antiquey, too. Even the box had an old-fashioned feel to it.

The letter said to keep the box, but why? To send it off? To who?

I decided to stash the box, the pouch, and the letter under my bed for now. I put the bracelet on my desk, opened my laptop, and tried to FaceTime my dad.

He didn't answer.

I ran to the living room and called him from the landline. I got his voice mail.

"Hi, Dad, it's me," I said. "Did you send me a bracelet? It's really pretty."

It was only like two p.m. in California, so he was at work. He's been really busy since he started his new job.

Often too busy to answer my calls.

I tried not to feel annoyed about his busyness. Brahm and I did spend a week with him in Santa Monica this summer, which was fun. And he's flying in for Brahm's bar mitzvah, of course. But would it be so hard for him to answer his phone?

I heard my mom's key in the door.

"Did you get me a bracelet?" I asked her.

"Sorry, sweetie?" She put down her grocery bags.

"Did you get me a bracelet for my birthday?"

"No. Did you want me to?"

"No, but I got one in the mail. Could be from Dad."

"Maybe. I don't know what he's getting you."

"I was hoping for a phone."

"It better not be a phone," she muttered. "You're too young for a phone."

"A lot of kids in my grade have phones," I pointed out.

She shook her head. "Studies link getting a phone too young to addiction and negative effects on brain development—"

"Why don't you care about Brahm's brain?"

"I do, but he's older."

Whatever. I walked over to Brahm, who was still reciting his Torah portion in the living room.

"What about you?" I asked. "I'm guessing the bracelet isn't from you?"

He glared at me and made a whole show of turning off his audio. "What about *I'm busy* don't you get?"

"So you didn't get me a bracelet for my birthday?"

"I didn't even know it *was* your birthday."

I sighed. "Forget it."

I went back to my room and sat down at my laptop to start my homework. The laptop was a hand-me-down from Brahm because he got a new one from his school this year. Even though I didn't have a phone, at least I could FaceTime and text on the computer.

I had one new message.

Dad: Sorry I missed your call, Becca! Busy at office. Did not send bracelet. But I was wondering what to get you—any ideas?

Okay, so the bracelet wasn't from him.

Who else could have sent it? I looked over at Twinkle, and he blew an air bubble in my direction. My fish was my only friend. Too bad he couldn't play story-a-thon.

Wait. Was it possible that Harper had sent me the bracelet? Maybe she'd mailed it before our fight? Or maybe she'd dropped it off as an apology gift? A peace offering!

If I wore the bracelet to school tomorrow, Harper would see it, throw her arms around me, and say she was so happy I forgave her. Everything would go back to normal, and Harper would come for my birthday after all.

I picked up the bracelet. It was kind of stretchy, so I was able to slip it onto my wrist. Pretty. Somehow, I felt better already.

The next morning, I spotted Harper and Georgette as soon as I stepped into the schoolyard.

I needed Harper to see that I was wearing the bracelet. I hurried over—casually—and stood a little behind them.

I saw Georgette notice me and elbow Harper.

I froze for a second. Then I lifted my hand—the hand wearing the bracelet—and waved. "Thank you?" I said, a question in my voice.

"For . . . ?" Harper asked coolly, looking at my hand.

"For the bracelet?" I said. "Is this from you?"

"No," she said.

"Oh."

"What is she talking about?" Georgette asked under her breath.

"She thinks I got her a bracelet," Harper murmured.

"Did you?" Georgette asked.

Harper picked at her thumbnail. "No, it's not from me, Becca. Sorry." She turned back to Georgette and whispered something.

I felt my cheeks flame. And more hives forming.

Fine, Harper didn't want to be best friends anymore. Or friends even. But did she have to be mean? Did we have to be enemies now?

"Miss Singer, you're holding up the line," Principal Bort snapped.

"Sorry," I said. Cheeks still burning, I hurried inside and headed up the stairs to my classroom.

Ms. Michaels wasn't there yet. As I walked to my desk, I heard the Three Es whispering.

"What's on her face?" Emma asked.

"Is that why she didn't come back to class yesterday?" Elizabeth asked.

"Did you hear that Harper ditched her?" Elijah added.

Great. They all knew what had happened.

I would spend the rest of the year completely alone. People would hide under their desks as I walked by, avoiding me. I would play Two Square by myself at lunch, but I would call it One Square.

I was a social pariah.

I slumped into my seat and touched the beads on my new bracelet.

Who had sent it?

If it wasn't my mom, or my dad, or my brother, or Harper . . .

I thought about the mysterious note that had come with the bracelet, and tried to remember its exact words.

Because you're blue . . . the bracelet is now for you. Something like that?

I frowned. Was it really possible that the bracelet had been sent to me because I was sad? Wasn't that what *blue* meant?

What else had the letter said?

Speak one wish to make it true.

Hmm. If I made a wish on the bracelet, the wish would come true?

It seemed silly, but it couldn't hurt to try, right?

What did I want to wish for?

I looked around the room. Well. It was obvious. I wanted friends.

I closed my eyes and thought: *I wish I had friends. Not just one friend. But lots and lots of friends. So many friends.*

Nothing happened. Not that I was really expecting anything to happen.

Although the note had said that I had to speak my wish.

So very quietly, I whispered, "I wish everyone wanted to be my friend."

And that, Addie, is when everything changed.

* 4 *

Make It True

The bracelet tightened around my wrist.

The lights in the classroom flickered, and a rush of air hit my skin.

I checked to see if someone had opened a window, but they hadn't.

Suddenly, my whole body felt like it was glimmering. Sparkling. But no—my arms were just covered in goose bumps. The bracelet was glowing and warm on my wrist.

Elizabeth twisted around and stared at me. The purple tiara she was wearing glittered under the fluorescent light.

I waited for her to turn back around again, but instead she asked, "Did you see *How to Dress Like a Royal* last night?"

There was only a white wall behind me. "Are you talking to me?" I asked.

"Of course! Did you?"

"No," I said. "Is that a new show?"

"Yeah, and it's fun. And they put everyone in crowns and that's why I wore this today." She adjusted the tiara on her head.

"It's very sparkly," I said.

"Do you want to try it on?" she asked eagerly.

Huh? "Your tiara?"

"Yes. Try it on!" She took it off her head and held it out to me.

"We're not supposed to share hats or brushes since last year's lice outbreak . . ."

Yes. I really mentioned lice. That's how skilled I am at making new friends.

"Oh, come on," Elizabeth said.

"You should totally try it," Elijah added.

"Try it!" Emma chimed in.

I was unclear about what was happening and why. But they all really wanted me to try on the tiara, and a tiara wasn't a hat or a brush, so . . .

I placed the tiara on top of my head.

"Gorge," Elijah said.

"Purple is your color," Emma said.

"You are a total queen," Elizabeth said.

"Thank you?" I said. I was so confused. I took off the tiara and handed it back to Elizabeth. Was it possible that my wish . . .

No. Impossible.

"Becca," I heard from my left.

I turned to see Shep looking at me.

"Yes?"

He had never spoken to me before.

"Can I show you what I drew today?" he asked.

"Sure?"

He pulled a piece of paper out of his backpack and put it on my desk. It was a drawing of a bat. A hyperrealistic bat.

It was really good. And super creepy. And why was he showing it to me?

"What do you think?" he asked.

The bat. The tiara. Something weird was definitely going on. Could it be . . . ?

No. That was ridiculous.

"Hello," Ms. Michaels said, walking into the classroom. "I'm pleased to see *everyone* is here and *on time* today." She glanced around the room, and her gaze landed on me.

Uh-oh.

"Becca!" Ms. Michaels said happily. "Good morning, Becca!"

Good morning, Becca?

Yes. I did not mishear. She said, "Good morning, Becca."

All the kids in the class turned around to look at me.

I tensed up like I was made of stone.

Then I realized Ms. Michaels was probably waiting for my homework. Right. Of course. Because I hadn't brought it yesterday.

"I have my homework," I said, my voice shaking. "Yesterday's too."

"Wonderful," she said, smiling. "Pass everything up, please."

I took out the worksheets and passed them up. Ms. Michaels glanced at them quickly. "These are terrific!" she exclaimed. "*Thank you* for bringing them in, Becca!"

Everyone looked as surprised by her words as I was.

"Three cheers for Becca!" Ms. Michaels said. "Come on, everyone! Hip, hip, hooray!"

"Hip, hip, hooray! Hip, hip, hooray!" everyone in the class chanted.

Was she being sarcastic? Yes, she had to be. She was making fun of me for finally bringing my homework.

I blushed harder. My teacher was making fun of me!

"Okay, class, time to *focus*," Ms. Michaels said. She turned and faced the whiteboard.

"You can have it," Shep whispered to me.

"What?" I whispered back.

"The drawing. You can have the drawing. If you want it. Or I can make you another one. Of whatever you want. I draw every animal. Do you like mice?"

"I don't like seeing them in my apartment, but otherwise they're kind of cute," I told him.

"I'll draw you one next time," he said.

Did he feel sorry for me that Ms. Michaels was making fun of me?

Yes. That had to be it.

I put the drawing in my notebook and turned to face the whiteboard. And the bracelet continued to glow on my wrist.

When the bell rang, I reluctantly reached for my lunch bag. Maybe instead of going to the cafeteria I would eat in the library. Or I could lock myself in the bathroom again. That would be better than sitting alone.

I glanced up to see the Three Es looming over my desk.

"Come to lunch with us!" Emma said.

"Me?" I asked.

"Of course!" Elijah said.

I wouldn't have to sit alone in the cafeteria!

As I walked down the hall with the Three Es, I glanced down at the pretty bracelet. This couldn't all be happening because of my wish. It was a coincidence. It had to be.

I sat at a table with the Three Es and spotted Harper across the room, sitting with Georgette. They were deep in conversation. I wanted to yell, *Take that, Harper! Other people want to be my friend! I don't need you!* But of course I didn't.

Harper turned to look at me. Our eyes locked, but I quickly looked away.

"Becca, what are you doing this weekend?" Emma asked between forkfuls of mac and cheese. "Want to come over?"

"Yeah, come hang out with us," Elijah said.

Did they really want to hang out with me outside of school?

"Actually," I said slowly. "It's my birthday on Saturday."

"It is? Fun! Are you having a party?" Elizabeth asked.

"I was, but . . ." I stopped. No need to go into it. "Should I?" I tried. I suddenly got sweaty.

"Of course you should!" Elizabeth exclaimed.

My mom *did* say I could invite other friends. "I guess I could have a party. Saturday. At five. Can you come?"

"Yes!" all three of the Es cried simultaneously.

WHAT. WAS. HAPPENING?

"What's the party theme?" asked Elijah.

"Tie-dye, maybe?" I said tentatively. "I got lots of white stuff. Pillowcases. T-shirts. Scrunchies. Pencil cases."

"A tie-dyed pencil case?" Elijah giggled. "Genius."

"Love it love it love it," Elizabeth said, nodding.

My bracelet felt hot. Was my wish working on the Three Es? It had to be. It couldn't be. But otherwise how was it possible that I suddenly had three friends who wanted to tie-dye on my birthday?

After we finished eating, Emma led the three of us out-side to the yard.

"I have to show you this new dance," she said. "It's wild. There's lots of hip popping and body rolls."

I did not know what either of those things meant.

"Watch and learn, darlings," Emma told us.

Elijah and Elizabeth copied her exactly.

I tried but was terrible at it. I literally tripped over my shoelace. I cringed, waiting for the Three Es to banish me back to the cafeteria.

But they laughed—with me, not at me—and helped me up. I took a bow. "Thank you, thank you."

"You're funny," Elijah said to me.

You know what? I *am* funny! Or at least, I've always thought so. It seemed like no one else noticed until that moment. And it was nice to hear. Harper never told me I was funny. Even pre-Georgette.

I bowed again, and they laughed even harder.

"Love your bracelet," Emma said. "Is it glowing?"

It *was* glowing.

"It's new," I said. "So . . . maybe it's a glow-in-the-dark bracelet . . . or I guess a glow-in-the-*light* bracelet."

Everyone laughed again. Okay, that one wasn't even my best comedic work. And they still laughed!

"Back to it," Emma said. "One, two, three, pop! One, two, three, pop! Now twirl!"

Mid-twirl, I spotted Harper out of the corner of my eye. She was talking to Georgette, but she stopped to wave at me.

The next thing I knew, Harper had left Georgette and was in front of me.

"Hi?" I asked. Was she really here, or was I dizzy from all the twirling?

She lowered her voice. "Can we talk?"

"We're in the middle of learning a dance," Emma pointed

out. "It's an actual dance from an actual music video, and Becca has only learned the first six moves. It's going to take all her concentration."

"Oh," Harper said, picking her thumbnail. "I can come back when you're done."

"No, no, it's okay," I said quickly, and turned to the Three Es. "I won't be long."

"Come back soon!" Elijah called out.

We walked a few feet away, and Harper looked down at the ground. "So . . ."

My bracelet felt extra warm. Almost hot. Ouch! "Yes?" I said, shaking my arm out.

"I'm sorry for yesterday," Harper said, looking into my eyes. "I don't know why I was so mean. Silly. Of course I want to be friends."

I straightened up. "You do?"

She nodded. "Best friends."

"But what about all the things you said?" I asked, my heart racing. "About us going different ways. About us not liking the same things. About plants."

She hung her head. "Forget everything I said, okay? I want you to be my best friend. I miss you. Please? Can we still be best friends?" she pleaded.

"But why are you changing your mind?" I asked. "Is it

just because other people want to be friends with me now?"
Is it because of the bracelet? That's what I was thinking. But
I couldn't say it. Plus I still hadn't totally wrapped my head
around the bracelet being magic. *Was* it magic? Did I even
want it to be magic? Or did I want people to like me for me?

"I want to be friends. Best friends," Harper said firmly.
"Can I still come to your birthday party?"

"I just invited the Three Es," I said.

"The more the merrier," she said. "It can be the five of us."

"And we're going to tie-dye," I said.

"Okay. We'll tie-dye," she said.

"Are you going to sleep over?" I asked.

"I . . . I could! If you want me to," she said quickly.

"What about your chess tournament?"

"It's . . . well . . . I'll skip it. I'll do it next time."

"Okay," I said. "If you're sure."

To be honest, I was a little weirded out. It felt like a boo-
merang with Harper. But I still wanted her at my birthday,
and I still wanted her to be my best friend.

The bell rang, and Harper gave me a hug. A hug!

"See you soon!" she called, and ran back to join a
confused-looking Georgette.

The Three Es smiled at me as I hurried over to them.

"All okay?" Elijah asked.

I nodded, dazed. The bracelet was still glowing and warm.

"Don't worry, we'll teach you how to do a body roll tomorrow," Emma said.

Harper wanted to be my best friend again. She was going to skip her chess tournament to sleep over.

The Three Es wanted to teach me to do body rolls.

Shep had offered me a drawing. A creepy drawing. But still.

I had made a wish—to have friends.

And it had . . . come true?

My hands were shaking. I had gotten a magical bracelet in the mail. I had made a wish! To have friends! And it worked!

This was better than a gift certificate. This was better than a phone.

This was the best present.

Ever.

* 5 *

You Too?

My mom met me outside school. "How was your day?" she asked.

"It was great, actually," I said.

"That's wonderful," she said, smiling and linking her arm through mine. "Does that mean you made up with Harper?"

"I did," I said. "She's coming over on Saturday."

"Wonderful. I knew it! Disagreements happen. People make up. It's normal. I'm so glad she's coming."

"And I invited three other kids from my class. That okay? Not to sleep over. Just to hang out."

Mom stopped and squeezed my shoulder. "That's terrific. I know it's scary and hard to make new friends, and I'm so proud of you for being brave and putting yourself out there."

I hadn't exactly put myself out there. I had just made a wish on a magical bracelet. On the other hand, I *was* making new friends, and that had to count for something.

I touched my bracelet. It was still warm and glowing.

How long would the magic last? Forever? What if I took off the bracelet? Would Harper decide she didn't want us to be best friends again?

"I love our walks home together," my mom said. "Do you want to get coffee?"

"Huh?"

"Well, you wouldn't get coffee, obviously, but you could get a hot chocolate."

"Sure," I said, surprised. "Starbucks?"

We turned the corner and headed down the block, stepped into the Starbucks, and ordered.

"Did I tell you that one of the teachers at my school gave notice yesterday?" Mom asked as we waited for our drinks. "She's becoming a real estate agent."

"No," I said, moving toward an empty table by the window.

I sipped my hot chocolate as my mom talked about whether or not she should get her staff ergonomic chairs. The coffee made her chattier than normal.

When we finished our drinks, we started walking toward our apartment.

"Oh, shoot," my mom said.

"What?"

"I chipped my nail."

"Want to go for a manicure?" I asked, completely joking.

"Good idea," she said.

"Wait, what? We can go for a manicure? Right now? Us?" I'd had one professional manicure in my lifetime, and it was when Harper's mom took us for Harper's birthday.

My mom smiled. "Sure. It'll be fun! And it is your birthday week." She took my hand and pulled me toward Oasis.

Starbucks. Chattiness. Manicures.

Wait. Was my mom trying to be my friend, too? OMG. Ha! She was! The magic was working on my mom! Did the magic work on everyone? It seemed like it did!

Was using magic to get people to be nice to me wrong? Probably. But it felt so right!

The salon was beautiful. There were pink leather lounge chairs, and it smelled like lavender and vanilla.

The technician told me to pick out the color I wanted and pointed to a rainbow wall of polishes. I picked out a lilac.

"I'll get the same color," my mom said. "We'll be twinsies!"

I almost laughed out loud. My mom had never used the word *twinsies* in her entire life. This magic was really something else.

We sat down in pink chairs next to each other, and our nail technicians sat across from us. I couldn't believe we were really here.

The manicurist, June, according to her name tag, was wearing bright red lipstick. She put my right hand in a bowl of hot water and rose petals.

"I'm just going to use the restroom," Mom said, standing up. "Be right back."

A customer sat down in the empty seat on the other side of me. She looked like she was in her early twenties, and she had super-straight blond hair cut into a blunt bob past her chin. She was wearing round diamond earrings, a white cashmere sweater, and a checkered scarf.

"That's a really unique bracelet," she said to me.

"Thank you," I replied.

"You should probably take the bracelet off during your manicure so you don't get cream all over it," she added.

"She's right," said June.

"Oh, no thank you," I said to both of them. I was not risking taking this bracelet off. Ever. What if the magic stopped working?

"Are you sure?" asked the blond woman. "You don't want it to get dirty."

"I'm sure, thank you," I said quickly.

"It's very beautiful," she added. "In fact—I'll give you twenty dollars for it."

Huh?

"Really?" I asked. Fancy Pants over there wanted my bracelet?

"Yes. Twenty dollars. What do you say?"

"I'm sorry, it's not for sale. It was a gift," I said. I didn't know from who, but it was still a gift.

"Thirty dollars, then."

Seriously? "I can't."

"Fifty. Final offer."

Fifty is a lot of money, but magic is priceless. And who was this person anyway? Was this a stranger's way of trying to be my friend? "Thank you for the offer, but I'm going to keep my bracelet," I said firmly.

"You're making a mistake," the blond woman said. She slid out of the chair and hurried out the salon's front door just as my mom was sitting back down.

I shivered. Something about that lady was odd. Who was she? Was she just trying to be nice or did she know about the magic? Was that why she wanted my bracelet?

I tried to forget about the blond woman as my mom and I got our nails done. I focused on our pretty, matching lilac color instead.

As we waited for our polish to dry, my mom glanced at her watch. "I need to pick up dinner. Chicken tonight?"

"Pizza?" I asked with a hopeful smile.

"Well . . ." She hesitated.

An opening! I pounced. "Please? Pretty please?"

She shrugged. "Why not. Birthday week!"

My heart sped up as Mom and I rode the elevator to our apartment. Was the magic going to work on my brother, too?

My mom unlocked the door.

"Brahm? Brahm?" I called out, running inside. "Brahm?"

He was wearing his earbuds again, pacing the living room.

He stared at me and blinked. And blinked again.

I waited for him to say something. Anything.

My bracelet was still warm and glowing—it was always warm and glowing. That had to mean it was working.

"What?" Brahm asked.

"Mom is ordering pizza for dinner," I said.

"What, is it a holiday?" he asked.

"Only the most important one. My birthday?"

He did not roll his eyes. He did not walk away. Instead, he laughed. Then he went back to practicing his Torah portion.

He wasn't rude but he wasn't exactly nice, either. So what did that mean?

I went to my room and turned on my laptop.

OMG. OMG. OMG.

I had nine new texts.

Nine.

Texts.

Harper: Can't wait for Sat!

Harper: 5 still good?

Harper: Or should I come earlier?

Harper: Can I come over after school tomorrow?

Elijah: Beccster! Adding you to our Three Es group text!

Emma: She has an e in her name! We can be the 4Es!

Elizabeth: 👍

Elijah: 🏃🏃🏃🏃

Elizabeth: Look at this quiz about what your hairstyle says about you.

I was on my first group text! And it was glorious!

I spent the next ten minutes texting back and forth with the Three Es—now Four Es!—and confirming tomorrow plus birthday plans with Harper.

Then I heard a knock on my door.

"Come in, Mom!"

The door opened. But it wasn't Mom. It was Brahm.

"Becs?" he asked. "Do you want to play cards?"

My brother had been the one to teach me to play cards back when I was little. Rummy 500. Spit. Crazy Eights. But we hadn't played in years.

"Yes!" I squealed.

I had homework to do, but I did not want to miss out on the magical opportunity to play cards with my brother.

"Fun!" my mom called out from the hallway. "Can I play, too?"

"Rummy 500!" I said. "Kitchen table!"

We ended up playing Rummy 1,000 that night.

We ate pizza while we played.

I loved every second of it.

My mom lost almost every hand, and my brother and I were tied until I won the last round with a set of aces.

"Woot!" I cried out.

I am pretty sure they didn't let me win. But not completely sure.

After I helped clear the table, I went back to my room. Outside my window, I saw Doodles the parrot flying around in the courtyard.

Would Doodles be nice to me now?

Doodles hovered outside my window. "Get lost!" she squawked. "Go away, Becca!" She flapped her wings angrily.

The parrot clearly still hated me.

I studied Twinkle. The fish wasn't treating me any differently, either. He was still mostly ignoring me.

So the magic worked on people but not animals. Or at least not on parrots and fish.

And how far did the magic reach? Five feet? Ten? The whole city? The whole world?

How could I test it out?

I sat at my desk and tried to FaceTime my dad.

No answer.

I texted him.

Hi Dad! You around? Call or FaceTime me?

If the bracelet's magic worked through the internet, then I'd hear from him, right?

I waited for him to call back. And waited some more.

He didn't call back.

So the magic didn't work on my dad. He must have been too far away.

Oh well. It worked on my mom and my brother and on everyone at school. That was something.

I studied the bracelet and thought about the letter it had come with. Hmm. Did "speak one wish to make it true" mean that the bracelet only worked once? Or could I wish for other stuff? I bounced up and down in my seat. Ooh, what if I got more wishes? What else did I want?

So many things!

"I wish I had a million dollars!" I called out.

I waited. Nothing happened. No gust of wind. No tingles. No piles of money popping up beside me.

Maybe a million dollars was too big an ask? I decided to try something smaller. "I wish I had an iPhone," I said.

Again nothing happened. No tingles, no wind, no iPhone magically appearing on top of my homework.

The friend magic had worked pretty much immediately. So I guessed that meant I only had one wish.

All right.

I smiled to myself. At least I had made a pretty good one.

✶ 6 ✶

The More the Merrier

The next morning, the bracelet was still glowing and warm on my wrist as I ate the chocolate chip pancakes I had requested for breakfast.

"What should I pack you for lunch?" my mom asked me. "Tofu and broccoli again?"

"Actually," I said through a mouthful of deliciousness. "Could I get a grilled cheese sandwich from the cafeteria?"

"Sure," she said.

My mom was saying yes to everything! And Brahm gave me a high five before he left for the day. A high five!

When Mom dropped me off at school, the Three Es immediately rushed over to greet me in the yard.

"Love the sweatshirt," Elijah said.

I was wearing the same tie-dyed sweatshirt I had been wearing on Monday.

"I'm wearing mine," Harper said, jumping in beside me. "We made matching ones," she told the group.

We had. And it was her first time wearing hers to school. But at least she was wearing it.

The whole crew of us walked toward the door.

I had a crew!

No, no, no. I didn't just have a crew. I had a crew that I was THE LEADER of.

"Put away your phone, Miss Mehta," Principal Bort said to Harper when we reached the door.

"Your backpack zipper is open, Miss Ono," Principal Bort said to Emma.

"Becca!" he said to me.

I was kind of shocked he knew my first name.

"Yes?" I said, waiting for him to tell me to tie my shoe-laces or something.

"It's so great to see you!"

Harper, Emma, Elizabeth, and Elijah stared at me, wide-eyed.

"Um, thank you," I said.

Harper, Emma, Elizabeth, and Elijah all walked into the building, but Principal Bort hovered in the doorway with me, like he wanted to chat.

"Tell me, Becca, do you knit?" he asked me.

"What?"

"Do you knit? I've taken up knitting. It's very calming. I'm working on a scarf right now. I'll bring it in tomorrow to show you."

Did Principal Bort want to be my friend? OMG. He did. Forget teacher's pet—I was going to be principal's pet.

"Sure, Principal Bort," I said. "I would love to see it."

"Please," he said. "Call me Mort."

"Okay . . . Mort."

Mort Bort? I tried my hardest not to laugh.

"Becca," Principal Bort—uh, Mort—went on, "would you tell me about that game you kids all play at recess? With the ball and squares?"

"Two Square?"

"Yes! That's it! How does it work?" The line behind me was starting to get long.

"Two kids throw a ball back and forth on the ground. It can only bounce once in the square or you're out."

"Oooh, fascinating. Have you ever played capture the flag? Now, that's an enjoyable game. I used to play it as a child. I was excellent at it. Not as good as Sally Jenkins. That girl was a capture-the-flag titan."

The bell rang. "Should we keep this line moving, maybe?" I suggested. "I don't want everyone to be late."

He nodded. "Yes, good thinking. See you, Becca!"

I hurried to class. Was Ms. Michaels going to be angry that I was late?

I opened the classroom door carefully.

"Hi, Becca!" Ms. Michaels said. "Come on in. So glad *you* could make it!"

This time I knew she wasn't being sarcastic—she had a huge smile on her face.

"Yay, Becca!" the kids who were already there cheered as I made my way to the back of the class.

"Wait, Becca?" Ms. Michaels said. "Why don't you move up here?"

"Up where?"

"Up to the front of the class! *Right* in front of me." She glared at Jeremy, a kid who currently sat in the front row. "Can you take Becca's seat in the back, *please*?"

"But I like this seat—"

"*Move it*, Jeremy!" she said, hurrying him along with a hand motion.

I slipped into my new desk. Willow Morales was sitting next to me. There were three novels piled on her desk. She read whenever there was a break.

"Here you go, Becca," Shep said, hurrying over and handing me a drawing. It was a very detailed mouse. "I hope you like it."

"Thank you!" I told him. So thoughtful that he'd remembered the mouse.

The rest of the kids eventually made their way inside the classroom. They all said hi to me as they took their seats. I loved the new normal.

Ms. Michaels closed the door. "Time for the spelling quiz," she said.

Spelling quiz? My stomach dropped. Oh no. With all the card playing last night, I had totally forgotten to study.

Ms. Michaels began reciting a list of words that we had to write down on a sheet of paper.

My heart hammered. I gripped my pencil as I wrote.

Sure, Ms. Michaels was liking me lately, but she wasn't going to like me if I got all the answers wrong.

Which I totally did. Because I hadn't studied.

"Hand your papers up!" Ms. Michaels called. We all passed them up. "Now, everyone read quietly while I grade the quizzes," she added.

Willow happily started reading one of her books. When she saw me watching her, she smiled. I was about to smile back when Ms. Michaels appeared at my desk, graded exam in hand.

Uh-oh.

"Here you go, Becca!" she said.

I accepted the test with clammy palms and checked out the grade.

Instead of THIS IS TERRIBLE WHY DIDN'T YOU STUDY, what Ms. Michaels had written was:

Good enough! A+! AHAHAHAHAHAHA.

Do you know how many mistakes I made on that quiz? So many!

I spelled *prominent* with an *a*.

I spelled *meticulous* without the *o*.

I was pretty unmeticulous.

But I could have spelled my name wrong and still gotten an A-plus.

This was getting wild.

At lunchtime, I stood in line for the hot lunch, excited.

The lunch lady, Ms. Debno, was in her twenties and wearing a bun. She smiled at me and gave me an extra helping of fries with my grilled cheese.

"Thank you!"

"Anything for you, darling," she said.

When I sat down at the table, it wasn't just the Three Es and Harper who wanted to sit with me. Daisy, Zuri, Corinne, and a bunch of other fifth-graders were crowding around me, too.

"I was sitting next to Becca!" Elizabeth said.

"No, I was!" Corinne argued.

I was a little squished in my seat, but I wasn't going to complain, was I? No, I was not.

I noticed that Georgette, horrible Georgette, was watching longingly from across the cafeteria. Now she wanted to hang around me, too?

Ha!

"Can I come to your party?" Daisy asked. "I heard it's going to be super fun."

"Absolutely," I said.

She smiled big, showing her pink braces. "Hurrah!"

"Me too?" asked Zuri, Daisy's best friend.

"Me too!" said Corinne.

"I want to come!" said a kid whose name I didn't even know.

"You can all come!" I called out happily.

How many people had I invited exactly? I wasn't sure. But my mom had told me to invite more people, hadn't she? She'd said the more the merrier!

A huddle of third graders stared at me as I left school that afternoon with Harper.

"Hi, Becca," one of them said. They all giggled.

"Hi," I said back.

"Omigod, she talked to us," another one said.

"I rescued her from the bathroom on Monday," a third one said.

They all shrieked. "OMG!"

"No way!"

"You're a hero!"

"Thank you!" I called out to the girl who'd saved me.

They all shrieked even louder.

"How did you become such a rock star?" Harper asked, linking her arm through mine.

"I'm not really a rock star," I told her.

"You totally are. Everyone wants to be friends with you."

I smiled. It was true. But all I really cared about was that Harper—my best friend—was coming over.

"Mom, can we get cupcakes on the way home?" I asked when my mom met us outside.

"Sure," she said.

Harper waggled her eyebrows. "That's new."

"A lot is new," I said with a laugh.

"So what should we do?" I asked when Harper and I were in my room, eating our cupcakes.

"Do you want to do story-a-thon?" she asked.

"We can do something else," I said.

"No, no, it's fine. Get some paper. You start."

"Okay," I said, taking out a piece of printer paper and starting to write. "Once upon a time, there was a brilliant, brave, and hilarious queen." I nodded to Harper.

"Who was the most brilliant, brave, and hilarious queen who ever was," she said.

Yay, she was doing it! I'd missed this so much. "The queen ruled over the magical land of . . . Yew Nork."

She didn't laugh. Instead she said, "Which was very, very magical."

"Yes. Right. Yew Nork was usually peaceful and calm, except for once a year, on Yew Near's Eve, when at the stroke of midnight, the evil witch of Yew Nork appeared."

"And she was never late," Harper said, and then waited for me to continue.

Right. Right.

We kept going for about ten more minutes.

"Flickers of lightning danced between the evil witch's fingers as she unleashed a powerful spell on the unfortunate royal architect," I said. I waited for Harper. I looked up and realized she was on her phone. "Harper?"

"Sorry, say that again?" She was still on her phone.

"Flickers of lightning danced between the evil witch's fingers as she unleashed a powerful spell on the unfortunate royal architect," I repeated.

"Um, because the witch was terribly evil, and the architect was very unfortunate," she said, finally paying attention. Kind of.

"There was a flash of magenta smoke and a loud POOF! and when the smoke cleared, the architect had turned into a purple, shiny, scaly dragon and she flew right over the Hudson River!" I waited for Harper.

She looked up from her phone. "Sorry, can you repeat that?"

I put the paper down. "We can stop," I said. Her heart clearly wasn't in this. She wasn't adding anything to the story—she was basically just repeating what I said.

"No, let's keep going," she said, picking at her thumbnail. "I know you like this."

"But you don't," I said. "Or you don't anymore. We can do something else. What do you want to do?"

"Play chess?" she asked.

"Oh. I don't have a chessboard," I said. "I can get one, though. But I don't know how to play."

We looked at each other. We used to have so much to talk about. We used to have so much in common. How had that changed?

"Um . . ."

"Well . . ."

"Want to look at Friendstagram?" she asked.

"Okay," I said.

She showed me her phone and started scrolling really fast. "I have thirty-four friends. And I post videos and pictures . . . Let me take one of us." She snapped selfies of us and then went to work adding filters.

My mom knocked on the door.

"Harper, your sitter is here to get you," my mom said.

"Okay," Harper said, jumping up. "I'll text you later, Becca!"

As I walked Harper to the door, I felt out of sorts. All I'd wanted was for things between us to feel normal again. And they did.

But also not.

* 7 *

Staying Dry

M om?" I said at dinner. (We were having pizza again. So much pizza. I was going to turn into a pizza. Not that I was complaining.) "I invited a few more people to the party on Saturday."

"How many more people?" she asked.

"Like, ten?"

"Ten people in total?" she asked.

"No, ten people more than yesterday," I said.

"How many in total?" she asked.

"Fifteen," I said.

"Fifteen people . . . in here?" She motioned around the living room.

"Yeah," I said.

Her eyes widened. "Are we feeding all these people?"

"I guess?"

She took a deep breath. "Okay. I can order some pizzas. And a birthday cake."

"A good one," I said. "With lots of chocolate. And we can do tie-dye?"

Mom nodded. "And we can all watch a movie," she suggested. "Something classic! Have you seen *The Princess Bride*?"

"I'll be in charge of popcorn!" my brother said.

Last year, my brother slept over at his friend Liam's house on my birthday while my mom did yoga in her room and Harper and I streamed Netflix.

This year would be a little different.

After dinner, I checked my laptop.

I had fifty-seven texts.

From the Three Es. From Daisy and Zuri. From Corinne. From Harper.

Harper: How would you feel about inviting Georgette to your party? She really wants to come.
Harper: Like really, really.

Corinne: Heyyyyyyy

Daisy: 😺 Do you like headbands?

Zuri: 🎉🎂

Georgette: Hi Becca. How are you?

Elizabeth: Check out this quiz! What your favorite dessert says about you.

Elijah: I like cake, which means I'm a great listener.

Emma: Liking pie means I'm flaky! LOL.

Georgette: Wondering what you're doing on Saturday? Wanna hang out?

Harper: Any way you can invite her? Would mean so much to her!

Elizabeth: Check out this quiz: What your favorite shoes say about you!

Elijah: OMG watch this Friendstagram dance video. It's the best. We'll practice tomorrow!

Emma: LOVE IT. Practicing now!

Elizabeth: Do you like it, Becca? ☺

I could barely keep up with the texts.

I decided not to respond to Georgette. I didn't want her at my party. I just didn't.

But I clearly needed to get on Friendstagram.

I found my mom in the kitchen doing some paperwork.

"Mom? Can I get a Friendstagram account?" I asked.

She grimaced. "Well . . . I don't know . . . I don't like the idea of you being on social media."

"A lot of people are on Friendstagram. Please can I? Pretty please?" I made my eyes really big and innocent like.

"It's not a big deal," Brahm called from the living room. "I'll help her with it."

"You will?" I asked.

"Sure," he said.

Mom sighed. "I guess there's no real harm. But your account has to be private and you can only approve people you know in real life. Deal?"

"Deal," I said. Yay! I raced into the living room, where Brahm was sitting on the couch.

"Help," I said to him. "I've seen people use it, of course. I was watching Harper on it today but . . . what exactly is Friendstagram?"

"It's like Instagram and Facebook," he explained. "You post pictures and videos, and people ask to be your friend. You can have an account on a computer, but most people post from their phones. Let me take a few pictures of you, and then we can set it up."

He took some shots of me in my room, posing with Twinkle in his fishbowl.

He took some shots of me in his room, leaning against his striped wallpaper, which he said would look cool.

And he was right! It did.

He even snapped some selfies of us together, making silly faces.

Then Brahm started an account for me on my laptop. I chose a photo of myself with the striped background as my profile picture. Next, Brahm added a fun pic of me with Twinkle as my first post.

"Now you need to request a few friends. I'll friend you to start you off."

Hurrah! My first Friendstagram friend. I accepted Brahm's request, then scrolled through his posts. There were pictures of him with his friend Jacob, his friend Liam, his friend Megan.

My brother really did have a lot of friends. I wondered how he did it without the help of a bracelet.

I typed Harper's name in the search bar and found her account right away. I requested her and almost immediately she accepted it. I scrolled through her pictures—she'd already posted a photo of the two of us from today. But before that, there were tons of pictures of her and Georgette. At last week's chess tournament. At Georgette's apartment. At Harper's apartment. They really had become best friends, and I hadn't even noticed. Or maybe I had, but I'd pretended not to.

Next I friended the Three Es. I watched the dance video that they'd wanted me to watch and practiced it around my room.

The next time I checked the clock, it was almost seven. I decided to jump in the shower, since I hadn't showered the night before.

In the bathroom, I turned on the water, stepped into the tub—and panicked.

What if the water washed off the magic? I jumped out, half-wet. Thankfully my wrist was still dry.

Maybe I shouldn't shower. People seemed to like me no matter what. Would it matter if I was smelly?

Then I had a better idea. I could take the bracelet off. It wasn't like I had any friends to make *in* the shower. As soon as I was out, I'd slip the bracelet on, and the magic would be back.

I gently, very gently, tried to push the bracelet over my hand.

But my hand was too big.

Hmm. It wasn't coming off. How had I gotten it on if I couldn't get it off?

I paused. Should I even risk taking it off? What if I did and the magic stopped completely?

Maybe I could cover the bracelet with a shower cap. Yes! Brilliant! I searched everywhere in the bathroom, but I couldn't find one.

What else would work? Plastic wrap? Yes, plastic wrap!

I threw on my robe and ran out to the kitchen, got out the plastic wrap, ripped off a piece, and started shrink-wrapping it to my wrist.

My mom appeared in the doorway. "Why are you dripping wet in the middle of the kitchen?"

"I don't want my bracelet to get wet," I explained.

"Oooookay," she said. "Hey, let's do something fun after you shower. I can make tea, and we can listen to music! Do you know what Lilith Fair was? Or do you want to try one of my nighttime meditations?"

Friend Mom didn't seem to care that it was almost my bedtime.

"I have to finish my homework," I said. "But maybe tomorrow?"

She nodded, but I could tell she was disappointed. "Be careful not to slip."

I wiped up the puddle I'd made and then hurried back to shower, very, very carefully.

☆ 8 ☆

Out of Control

When I walked into the schoolyard on Thursday morning, I noticed something odd.

At least half the kids were wearing tie-dye. Like I had worn yesterday.

Oh, wow. I had started a trend!

Another was that everyone wanted to talk to me.

"I brought hummus for lunch today, Becca!" cried a fourth-grade boy. "Do you like hummus? I'll share!"

"Becca, can you come over after school?" a first grader asked, pulling on my sleeve. "My mom said I could invite you. Louie, my schnauzer, wants to meet you!"

"Becca? Do you play pickleball?"

"Becca, will you accept my Friendstagram request?"

Everyone was crowding around. It was a bit claustrophobic, if you want to know the truth.

"Becca?" Principal Bort called from the school entrance, motioning me forward.

"Excuse me, I need to get through," I told the mob of kids, hurrying to the door. "Good morning, Principal Bort."

"It's Mort," he reminded me. "And look what I brought to show you!" He pulled out a half-finished green-and-blue scarf. It had a bunch of large holes in it. "Not bad, huh?" he said. "My therapist recommended I try knitting to de-stress."

Did I want to know about Principal Mort and his therapist? Not really.

Thankfully, the bell rang, and I raced to my classroom.

"This *morning*," Ms. Michaels said as I took my seat, "I want everyone to read *independently*."

"Awesome!" cheered Willow.

I love independent reading, too. I stood up to get a book from the class library, when Ms. Michaels motioned for me to pull my chair up to her desk.

"I have to tell you, Becca," she said. "You remind me of myself when I was a student. Quiet, but you have a real presence. People are drawn to you. Have you thought about acting? Do you know I was an extra in *Cats*?"

"I didn't," I said, imagining her in a cat costume and cringing.

She sighed. "I love to sing. Teaching was my backup plan. But here I am."

"Sorry," I said.

"Maybe one day I'll audition again. Do you want to see pictures of me onstage? I have them on my phone."

"Sure?" I said.

I could hear Willow giggling behind her book.

Once again, I walked with the Three Es to the cafeteria. I was excited to get mac and cheese and sit down with my friends.

As soon as we stepped into the cafeteria, I was mobbed.

"Becca, I made you a brownie. It has nuts in it, though. Oh no, you're not allergic, are you?"

"Becca, do you like meatballs?"

"Becca, do you want to play Monopoly?"

The kids were getting closer and closer, like zombies closing in.

"Becca, did you see my texts last night?" asked Georgette, pushing her way toward me.

I knew what she was talking about but pretended I didn't. "I got a lot of texts last night," I said.

"I sent them at about six," she said, reaching for me.

I twisted away from her and banged my elbow into a table.

"Ow," I said.

The people around me gasped.

The entire cafeteria got eerily silent.

Then everyone started screaming.

"Are you okay?" Emma cried.

"She's hurt! Becca's hurt!" Elijah yelled.

"Georgette!" Harper yelled. "What did you do?!"

My elbow did hurt, but I didn't want to make a big deal out of it. "I'm fine," I muttered.

"She looks upset!" someone shrieked.

"Call 911!"

"We need an ambulance!"

"Does anyone have a healing crystal?"

"I'm FINE!" I said, louder this time. "Can I just get some space?"

Finally, people started backing off, and I took a breath.

"I am so sorry, Becca," said Georgette, her face drained of color.

"What happened?" Harper asked her.

"It was an accident," Georgette said, her eyes filling with tears. "I swear. I just wanted to talk to her. I want to be invited to her party!"

"You hurt her!" Elizabeth cried.

"Can everyone calm down?" I said, wincing.

"I'll get you your lunch!" Emma said to me.

"No, no, I can get it," I said.

"No, no, *I'm* getting her lunch," Georgette said. "I insist."

"Okay, okay, you can get my lunch," I said. "Mac and cheese, please."

"On it," Georgette said, saluting me.

I sat down at a table, and everyone started jostling for the two seats beside me.

"That was my seat!" Emma said.

"No, it was mine!" Elizabeth said.

"I'm her best friend!" Harper said.

"I never get to sit next to her!" said Zuri.

I closed my eyes. I wanted them all to be quiet.

Sure, I'd wanted to have friends. But these people didn't give me a moment to myself. And they weren't even real friends. They just wanted to be my friend because of the bracelet.

If I took the bracelet off, would they still like me?

I shook my head. No. They wouldn't. They had never been interested in me before.

Even Harper would probably dump me again.

Then I wondered: Did it matter *why* they wanted to be my friend? Who knows why people want to be friends with each other? Sometimes it's because they've known each other a long time. Sometimes it's because they're in the same class. Sometimes it's because their parents are friends. Sometimes it's because they both like Legos and are too shy to talk to anyone else. In this case, it was because I was wearing a magic bracelet. What's the difference?

"Here's your lunch!" said Georgette, appearing with a tray of mac and cheese.

But just as she was putting it down, Emma was standing up, and the two of them collided.

The tray went flying.

My mac and cheese soared through the air like orange confetti and landed all over everyone in the vicinity.

There were shrieks.

"Oh no!"

"Becca's lunch!"

"That was not my fault!" called Emma.

Georgette burst into tears.

"I'll get you a new one!" said Daisy.

"No, I will!" said Elijah.

"I'll get my own lunch," I said, annoyed and, honestly, very, very hungry.

"We'll clean up the mess!" said Harper.

Georgette was still sobbing. "Now she's never going to invite me to her party!"

She was right about that at least.

I stormed over to the now-quiet lunch line. Shep was the only one in front of me. I took a deep breath and tried to calm down.

"Hi, Becca. I'm almost done with a snake picture for you," he said.

"Oh. Amazing," I said, focusing on him. "You're so good at drawing."

He blushed. "Thank you."

"Your drawings are so realistic. Does everyone ask you to draw stuff for them all the time?"

"Huh? No. Not really. I don't show people my stuff."

"Why not?" I asked.

"I don't know. I guess not everyone likes bats as much as I do. And no one ever asks to see them. I don't have as many friends as you do. I don't know why I showed you, to be honest." He shrugged. "I was scared to."

He was? "Well, I'm glad you did," I said. "Oh! Shep! Listen, I'm having a birthday party on Saturday. Can you come?"

"Saturday? Yes, I can!" He smiled.

"I'll text you the information."

"I don't have texts," he said.

Oh, right. I wasn't the only person without a phone. "I'll email it, then."

"Great. Thank you." He turned to Ms. Debno. "One turkey sandwich, please."

She smiled and handed it to him.

"Bye," Shep said to me. "See you in class. And at your party. And tomorrow." He picked up his tray and headed to the checkout.

I watched him walk to the other side of the cafeteria. He sat at the corner of a table by himself.

He was eating all alone? Didn't he have anyone to sit with?

"Becca!" said Ms. Debno. I turned back to her.

"Why did you send someone else to get your meal? Didn't you want to say hi? Are you upset with me or something?"

Wait, what? "I didn't send someone else. She wanted to get me lunch because I bumped my elbow and . . ."

Was this really happening?

The lunch lady sniffed, and her lower lip trembled. "I thought maybe you were mad at me."

"No, no, no. Of course not. But can I get a bowl of mac and cheese? Please."

"Sure. One bowl of mac and cheese. Can I give you something else? Anything. Oh! How about an oatmeal cookie?"

"There are oatmeal cookies on the lunch menu?"

She leaned closer to me. "No, but I made some for myself. And you should try one! Let me give you a delicious cookie."

"No thanks."

"Please! Take a cookie! You have to take a cookie."

"Okay, okay, I'll take a cookie. Give me the cookie!"

She smiled and put a bunch of cookies on my tray. They were golden brown with dark orange chunks of . . . raisins? I wasn't sure. Anyway, I probably wasn't supposed to take cookies from the lunch lady's personal stash. I mean, she wasn't a stranger, so I wasn't worried about being poisoned. But still. It seemed wrong. And the cookies did not look good.

"Try them," she said.

Right here? "I'm going to eat the mac and cheese first, if that's okay?"

"But I want to see if you like the cookie. Take a bite!"

I paused. I took a small bite.

It was gross. Like really, really gross. I fake smiled.

Her face fell. "What's wrong? You don't like it?"

"I'm not a big cookie fan," I lied.

"You don't like it! Oh no! That's terrible! I'm sorry! I'm so sorry!" She started to sob and her mascara smeared down her face.

"It's okay! Don't cry! It's delicious! I'll have another bite!

See! Look at me loving the cookie! I'm eating the cookie, I'm eating the cookie!" I shoved another four bites into my mouth and chewed. "Delish! Best cookie ever!"

Ms. Debno wiped her tears away with the back of her gloved hands. "Really?"

"Really," I said. "I'm going to check out now, 'kay?"

She nodded. "It's on me."

"No, please, my mom said she would pay for school lunches this week."

"I insist!"

I did not feel like fighting, so I thanked Ms. Debno, backed away from the counter, and hurried back to my seat. The Three Es, Harper, Zuri, Daisy, and Corinne all crowded around and asked me if I was okay.

I nodded, took one bite of mac and cheese, and felt a tap on my shoulder.

I turned around. Georgette was standing there, her eyes red from crying. "Harper and I cleaned up the mac and cheese," she told me. "I'm really sorry for everything."

I swallowed. "It's okay."

"Then can I come to your party?"

I sighed. "Yes, Georgette, you can come to my party."

She smiled and gave Harper a thumbs-up.

"Me too?" asked two random fourth graders who were hovering nearby.

"You too," I said. Why not?

I spent the rest of the day dodging my fans, aka every kid in school. In class, Ms. Michaels showed me at least sixty more of her photos, including a baby picture of her dressed as a sunflower.

I was exhausted by the time I met my mom in the yard. "Is it okay if I skip Hebrew school today?" I asked. "I'm really tired."

"No problem," she said. "I had a long day, too. I got into an argument with the school crossing guard. She was rude to one of the kids for no reason!"

That's when I noticed my mom's outfit. She was wearing light blue jeans, a gray T-shirt, and a red hoodie.

Which was exactly what I was wearing.

Exactly.

She linked her arm through mine.

"Did you copy my outfit?" I asked.

"Oh! Yeah!" She smiled. "I thought we could be twinsies again! Aren't we so cute?"

"Where did you even get those clothes?" I wondered. "Are they new?"

"Yup! I did some shopping on my lunch break! I wanted to surprise you."

I didn't want to tell her that she was weirding me out, but she was weirding me out. Did I want to be twinsies with my mother?

"I know what will perk us up," Mom said. "Want to try a Bikram yoga class?"

"No thanks."

"Oooh, maybe we should get matching haircuts?"

This was getting surreal. The bestie mom, the zombie friends, all Ms. Michaels' pictures. "No thanks. Can we just go home?"

"You know, I still need to buy you something for your birthday. What would you like? More tie-dye? A Lego set?"

I stopped. This was my chance. "What about . . . ?"

"Yes?"

"A phone," I said.

She hesitated. Then nodded. "Okay. I'll get you a phone."

My heart sped up. "An iPhone?"

"An iPhone," she repeated.

"Really truly?" I squealed.

"If it makes you happy . . . yes!"

"You're the best, Mom," I said. "So I can get it now?"

"Sure. Let's go to the store!"

I felt sorry for doubting the bracelet. It really was amazing.

As soon as I got home, I set up my new phone and added the Friendstagram app.

I logged in.

I had one hundred and sixty-seven friend requests.

One hundred and sixty-seven! Did I even know one hundred and sixty-seven people? Who were these people?

I scrolled through the requests. Kids from my grade. Kids from fourth grade. Kids from third grade. Were third graders allowed on Friendstagram? Did their parents know they were on there?

Did I even want third graders to follow me?

I looked over at Twinkle. He continued to swim around his bowl and ignore me. Good old Twinkle.

I called my dad.

I got his voice mail. "Hi, Dad! I got a new phone! Yay! So call whenever you want, okay? Love you!"

Sometimes I thought my dad didn't call me on the house phone that much because Mom might answer and they'd have to talk. So now that I had my own phone, would he call all the time?

"Who were you calling?" my mom asked, coming into my room.

"Oh. Just Dad," I said. "But I got his voice mail."

"He's probably at work. You know how he is when he's working. Forgets everyone else. Even his family."

My shoulders clenched. My mom never said stuff like that. You'd think that if your parents got divorced they'd always be talking badly about each other, but not my parents. It's not like they're best friends or anything. But I once overheard my mom tell Bubby that Mom's therapist said it was important for kids not to hear their parents bad-mouthing each other in a divorce. That's what friends are for, according to the therapist.

In this case, I did not want to be treated like a friend.

"He basically disappears," my mom continued. "Forgets that his responsibilities aren't just financial." She shakes her head. "Don't you agree?"

"Um . . . uh . . ."

She wasn't wrong. But I didn't like hearing it from her.

I hated that it felt like my dad was the only person in the world not reaching out to me. Everyone wanted to be my friend. Everyone except him.

I touched the bracelet. I wished the magic could travel to California.

I shook my head.

Speak one wish to make it true.

If only I had another wish.

✳ 9 ✳

Super Student

On Friday morning, all four hundred elementary school students and all the teachers were gathered in the gym. It was the big assembly. I was sitting crisscross applesauce on the floor, squished between Harper and the Three Es. Daisy, who uses a wheelchair, sat right beside us, and Georgette, Corinne, and Zuri sat on the floor behind me.

Principal Bort was standing on the stage. He had just finished writing our school action words on a large paper pad:

Perseverance! Creativity! Gratitude!

Kindness! Responsibility!

When he was done, he said, "And now it's time to announce the Super Student of the Week!"

Everyone froze. Who would it be?

But of course I knew. First of all, he was looking right

at me and smiling. And second of all, how could I not win? Come on. Everyone at school was obsessed with me!

"This week's Super Student is . . . Becca Singer!"

Even though I'd been expecting it, hearing him say my name still sent a thrill through me.

"Yay, Becca!" cried the Three Es.

Harper squeezed my arm.

Everyone cheered.

That's kind of an understatement. People didn't just cheer. They hollered. They shrieked. I don't think I'd ever heard that much noise in the gym—or anywhere. I was surprised the windows didn't break.

Normally the Super Student just stands up and waves and then sits back down.

So I stood up. And waved. Then sat back down.

But the cheering went on.

And on.

Then they started chanting: "Becca! Becca! Becca!"

I wasn't sure what to do. So I stood up again and waved again.

And now there was new chanting: "Speech! Speech! Speech!"

Mr. Bort leaned into the mic. "Becca, why don't you come up and say a few words?"

Everyone cheered even louder.

OMG. Super Students of the Week never went up onstage! Why did I have to go up onstage? What was I supposed to say?

The chanting continued.

"Becca! Becca! Becca!"

"Speech, speech, speech!"

I started to worry the chanting would never stop if I didn't go up. So I headed to the stage. The cheers got louder with every step.

Mr. Bort handed me the mic. "And while you're here," he said, "I'd like to present you with the scarf I made you!"

He handed me the scarf he had been knitting. It still had lots of holes in it and was shaped in a zigzag.

"Um, thank you," I said, putting it over my arm.

"Wear it!" he said eagerly.

It was at least ninety degrees in the gym. And the scarf wasn't so much a scarf as a knitted . . . thing. But okay. I wrapped it around my neck and took the mic.

"Thank you all so much," I said.

Now the cheers were deafening. I didn't know what else to say. Or do.

So I did what I've seen rock stars do on TV.

I stood onstage and raised my arms in a V over my head. V for Victory! I was killing it.

For a whole thirty seconds.

Because when I brought my arms down, I somehow knocked over the microphone stand, sending it crashing to the ground.

I ran to pick it up, tripped, and belly flopped onto the stage.

For a second, there was silence.

And I thought: *This is it. The magic cannot keep me safe from making a complete joke of myself. They are going to boo me off the stage.*

But someone started clapping again. And then so did everyone else. And they resumed their chanting: "Becca! Becca! Becca!"

I could do no wrong.

I stood up again, waved to the crowd, and started walking off the stage.

Then I spotted Shep in the back corner. Sitting by himself.

I thought of him by himself at lunch. And saying he had no one to show his awesome art to.

Out of the corner of my eye I saw the words Mr. Bort had written. *Perseverance! Creativity! Gratitude! Kindness! Responsibility!*

Was there a way I could use the magic in a different way? To be responsible? To be kind? Maybe to help someone else?

I turned around and approached the mic again.

"I'm back," I said.

More cheering.

"So while I really appreciate being Super Student of the Week, I'd like to nominate another student instead. Someone you may not all know, but who is super talented. Is that okay?"

Principal Bort hesitated. "I suppose," he said. "No one has ever done that before. But I don't see why not. Who would you like to nominate?"

"Would Shep Harris come up on the stage?"

The crowd was quiet. Everyone turned around, searching for Shep.

Shep looked up in surprise. *Me?* he mouthed.

"Yes!" I said. "Would you mind drawing something for us on Principal Bort's pad of paper? I think everyone should see what a talented artist you are!"

Shep's cheeks were bright red, but he was smiling. "Sure," he said, and came on up.

Principal Bort handed him the Sharpie.

"What should I draw?" Shep asked me.

I turned to the crowd. "What should he draw? Tell him your favorite animal!"

"A wiener dog!"

"An owl!"

103

"An octopus!"

I turned to Shep. "Can you draw an octopus?"

He nodded and started drawing.

As he drew, the kids oohed and aahed.

The octopus was extremely detailed, extremely creepy, and extremely impressive.

"Can he do another one?" someone called out.

"I don't mind," Shep said.

He started drawing an owl, and people clapped and cheered.

It felt so good to share the magic!

I took the mic and asked Principal Bort, "Now! What do you think about honoring a teacher, too?"

"Super Teacher of the Month?" he asked.

"I was thinking more like we could have a teacher showcase a talent . . ."

"Do you have anyone in mind?" he asked eagerly. "Should I show everyone the new scarf I've started knitting?"

"I'm sure it's a great scarf, but I was thinking of Ms. Michaels. She said she sings!" I turned to the audience. "What do you think? Want to come up and sing for us, Ms. Michaels? Something from that musical you were in?"

Ms. Michaels' eyes widened, and she jumped up. "I *accept*! I accept your invitation!" She hurried onto the stage, beaming. Maybe she'd be less grumpy now.

I remembered we were supposed to have a math test after the assembly, and I got a new idea. "One last thing," I said to Principal Bort. "This afternoon, instead of class, could we play outside? It's such a nice day!"

"I don't know . . ." he said. "What would everyone play?"

"Capture the flag?" I suggested. "Didn't you used to play that?"

He chuckled to himself. "True, true. Okay, students. Since it is such a nice day today, let's go out to the yard for a schoolwide game of capture the flag!"

"And can we have Popsicles?" I added, because I was on a roll.

Everyone held their breath.

He hesitated. "And Popsicles."

The cheering rocked the room.

"Thank you, Principal Bort," I said to him.

"Please, Becca. Call me Mort," he replied.

I handed Ms. Michaels the mic. She smiled at the crowd and made what I can only describe as a cat face. Then she meowed. Finally, she started singing, *"Macavity's a Mystery Cat: he's called the Hidden Paw . . ."*

Everyone was running around the yard, laughing and playing capture the flag. Ms. Debno was handing out Popsicles.

"You're amazing, Becca!" someone called as they ran by.

"Way to go, Becca!"

"Can't wait for your party, Becca!" (I was starting to get a little worried about how many people, exactly, I had invited.)

On the one hand, it was great to see everyone having fun because of something I had set in motion. Yay, me!

But on the other hand, all the attention and nice things people were saying felt kind of . . . empty. What was the point of having friends if they were all *fake* friends? What was the point of getting cheers if they were *fake* cheers? Sure, other people had friends for reasons just as random as my magic bracelet. Or almost as random. But no one was getting *this* much attention for no reason.

While everyone was busy in the yard, I wandered inside and into the library.

Willow was sitting at one of the tables, reading.

"Hi," I said. "How come you're not playing outside?"

"Just taking a break," she said. "It's too bananas out there. I mean, it's fun, but capture the flag isn't really my thing."

"Oh, sorry," I said.

"What you did for Shep was great, though. That was super nice of a Super Student."

"Thanks," I said, smiling. "Are you coming to my party tomorrow?"

"Oh! Am I invited?"

"I thought I had told everyone in our class to come . . . I hope I did . . ."

"I'll try to come, for sure," she said. "I don't always love crowds, but I'll come by for a bit. Thanks for the invite. I appreciate it."

"What are you reading?" I asked.

"Dork Diaries. It's so funny. Like, I-snort-laughed-my-water-across-the-table funny. Have you read it?"

I shook my head. "Not yet."

"It's not a real diary, of course. It's fictional, but there are all these drawings and it's about regular school stuff but like really funny, you know?" She gestured with her hands as she talked. "Do you like to read?"

"Yeah. Fantasies mostly. I like to write, too," I said.

"Cool! Are you writing something now?"

I thought of the story I had started with Harper, which hadn't really worked. "Uh, not right now."

"Well, I'd love to read something you wrote," Willow said.

She was so sweet. But would she still want to read something I wrote if I wasn't wearing the bracelet?

"Becca!" we heard kids calling from outside. "Where are you? Becca?"

"I better go," I said. "See you tomorrow?"

"See you then!"

I left the library with a wave.

"Time to light the Shabbat candles!" my mom called out that evening.

Brahm and I joined my mom in the kitchen. Shabbat is the Jewish day of rest—also known as the Sabbath—and it starts on Friday night and ends on Saturday night. We don't strictly observe the Sabbath or go to synagogue for it, but we do have Shabbat dinners every Friday. They make the night feel special.

Mom lit the two candles in the two silver candlesticks, waved her hands over the two flames, covered her eyes, and started saying the Hebrew prayer.

"*Baruch atah Adonai . . .*" she began.

I tried to focus and sing along with her. But I kept thinking about school that day. Even though it had been fun, something inside me felt sad. I couldn't put my finger on why. Everything was awesome, wasn't it? I was Super Student of the Week. I had used my power for good. I had a ton of friends. I was basically getting everything I wanted.

"*. . . L'hadlik ner shel Shabbat,*" my mom finished. Then she started on the blessing for the wine. She'd poured me and Brahm two glasses of grape juice in wineglasses, like always.

My thoughts kept tumbling around. Maybe it was just that my dad still hadn't called me back. Or that yeah, Harper was my best friend again, but things didn't really feel the same between us.

But I had another three hundred friend requests on Friendstagram! Everyone in the school who had an account had friended me. Including Ms. Michaels and Principal Bort! Some people from my apartment building had friended me, too. And some people who didn't even know me. I didn't accept their requests, since I had promised Mom I wouldn't.

But how had the magic worked on them if they had never met me? Did they just see their friends follow me and decide to do the same? Was that all Friendstagram was? A snowball effect?

It all felt a little bit, well, fake.

Would everything always feel fake?

I shook my head. If I decided I didn't want the magic anymore—one day, far off in the future—I would just take the bracelet off. That had to be the way to end it. I couldn't wish to undo the magic—since that was a second wish. No, I would squeeze my hand out of the bracelet and that would be that.

And anyway, I didn't want the magic to stop.

I was having a party!

I had a ton of friends!

I had an iPhone!

"Becca? Don't you want challah?" Brahm asked.

Oops. I had somehow missed the prayer over the challah, which was my favorite part.

Challah is a special braided bread loaf that's eaten on Shabbat. It's sweet and delish. I happily accepted the piece of challah Brahm handed me, and then we sat down at the table.

"Hey, Brahm?" I asked quietly while Mom took the chicken out of the oven.

"Yeah?"

"Does Dad call you a lot on your phone?"

"Barely," he said.

"He hasn't called me once. It is kind of annoying," I said. "And whenever I FaceTime him, he doesn't answer."

Brahm shrugged. "It's hard for him to FaceTime from work," he told me.

"I guess," I said. "I'm sure he'll call tomorrow, though. Since it's my birthday."

"Yeah, he'll call tomorrow," Brahm said. "For sure. Excited for your big party?"

"Yes," I said, my stomach fluttering. "A little nervous. But excited."

"Nothing to be nervous about," Brahm said. "What could go wrong?"

Ha. How about everything?

✳ 10 ✳

Happy Birthday to Me

When I woke up the next morning, the first thought I had wasn't about the magic bracelet. It was: *It's my birthday!*

But then my mom came into my room with a tray of chocolate chip pancakes with extra whipped cream. Then Brahm came in with a card he'd made himself. He had drawn a big ace of hearts on it and written *You are aces.*

Extra whipped cream! A homemade card! The magic was definitely at work.

Bubby and Zadie called to wish me happy birthday. And Harper called. But still no word from Dad. I was sure he would call at some point, though. Of course he would. He was busy, but not busy enough to forget his own daughter's birthday.

It was three hours earlier in California. So he still had lots of time.

Every few minutes, someone would text to wish me a happy birthday. I think I got three hundred text messages. And at least a hundred that read, *See you tonight!*

"Honey, do you still want to do the tie-dye?" my mom asked as we hung streamers on the living room wall.

"I do, but with so many people coming, I'm afraid the dye will get everywhere."

She nodded. "Maybe we'll just put out fabric markers and let people decorate the shirts and pencil cases. And we can play music and put out some games?"

"Sounds good. Thanks, Mom."

At a quarter to five, I was setting out the snacks when the buzzer rang. The first guest!

"Who is it?" I called into the intercom.

"Shep!"

"Come on up!"

I waited eagerly by the door.

"Hi!" I said when Shep appeared. "Thank you for coming!"

Instead of his sweatpants and school sweatshirt, he was wearing jeans and a button-down.

"Happy birthday," he said shyly. "Thank you for inviting

me. And for what you did yesterday. That was the nicest thing anyone has ever done for me."

I blushed. "Oh! No problem. I'm so glad."

"I made you a picture." He handed me a piece of paper with a red ribbon around it.

It was a drawing of me! I was wearing a tie-dyed shirt. "Oh, wow," I said. "I love it!"

"I heard you say we're doing tie-dye?" he asked. "I've never done tie-dye, but it sounds fun."

I felt a pang. "I think there might be too many people for tie-dye—" I started to explain, but the buzzer rang again.

This time it was Willow.

"I'm so glad you came!" I said, opening the door for her.

She handed me a small rectangular box. "Happy birthday, Becca."

"Aw, thank you!" I said, and set the gift aside.

The buzzer starting going off every minute. Brahm took over intercom duty so he could buzz people up.

Buzz!

The Three Es.

Buzz!

Jeremy.

Buzz!

Zuri and Corinne.

Buzz. Buzz. Buzz. By five past five, there was a *line* to get into the apartment.

"I think we need to get more pizzas," my mom said, her eyes the size of pizzas.

I spotted Harper and Georgette come through the door together, each carrying large, matching gift boxes.

"Oh, hello, Mrs. Singer," I heard Georgette say to my mom. "Thank you so, so much for inviting me! What a treat!"

I rolled my eyes. So Georgette was one of those polite-to-parents-but-mean-to-other-kids kids, which didn't surprise me. And that's not even my mom's last name.

I waited for my mom to tell Georgette to call her Lori, like she always did with my friends. But instead she said, "It's Ms. Berkowitz." I caught my mom's eye, and she winked at me.

By five fifteen, there were over one hundred people in the apartment. I wasn't sure how everyone fit. People were sitting on the couch, on the floor, and on the windowsills. People were spilling into the kitchen and the bedrooms, the laundry room, and even the bathroom.

And the gifts kept piling up. Boxes and boxes of gifts! I should have said no gifts, but I hadn't even thought of it. Also, who doesn't want gifts?

"Happy birthday, Becca!"

"Yay, Becs!"

"Best party ever, Becca!"

Wait, was that my six-year-old neighbor with her sax?

And was that my old babysitter, Rose?

There were so many people, talking, eating, designing T-shirts, doing handstands, I could barely move.

My brother had put on some music, but no one could even hear it.

The bowls of chips and popcorn were long gone. My mom had ordered five more pizzas.

"All these kids are your friends?" she asked, confused.

"Kind of," I said.

Because they weren't, really. They were here because they had to be. The magic was making them.

I saw Willow at the door. Oh no. Was she leaving? I tried to make my way over to her but couldn't squeeze through the huge crowd.

She was leaving!

I felt a lump in my throat.

This party wasn't turning out the way I'd imagined.

I looked around.

Packed house. Mess everywhere.

Pizza on the floor. Pizza on our couch.

All I had wanted was a quiet night at home with a good friend. I glanced at Harper, who was taking selfies with Georgette in the corner. I'd wanted to tie-dye. I'd wanted to do story-a-thon.

But instead I was crammed into my apartment with strangers who didn't really want to be here. And I didn't really want them here, either. What was the point in any of it?

Being surrounded by so many fake friends made me feel lonelier than ever.

I fingered my bracelet. Maybe it would have been okay to have a birthday with just me and my mom and brother.

I took a deep breath. Maybe I didn't want the magic anymore.

Trying not to think too hard about it, I very gently tried to push the bracelet up and off my wrist.

It was stuck.

I tried harder. I looked for the clasp—but remembered there wasn't one. I tugged on the bracelet, but it didn't budge. It was almost like it was glued to my wrist.

My heart sped up as something began to dawn on me—what if I could never take it off?

What if everyone wanted to be my friend forever? I would never know if anyone really liked me. Teachers would always give me A-pluses even when I didn't deserve them.

If I got married, my partner wouldn't really be in love with me!

Everything would be meaningless forever.

I tugged harder on the bracelet, but it wouldn't come off.

OMG. It *was* stuck. My heart started to race. My cheeks heated up. Was that a hive forming?

My magic bracelet had become a handcuff! I wanted—needed—it off this very second.

That's when I saw a familiar face in the living room. It was the fancy blond woman from the nail salon. She was standing by the window, wearing an expensive-looking denim jumpsuit. She was *here*? How? Why?

I felt creeped out seeing her, but I also felt relief. She wanted my bracelet. Maybe she could help me get it off.

She caught me looking at her and smiled a slow smile. She pushed through the crowd toward me.

"Ready to sell it to me now?" she asked, her voice low.

"Who are you?" I asked. "Why do you want the bracelet?"

"I'm just someone who knows what it can do," she said lightly, but her eyes were gleaming. She touched something at her collarbone, and I noticed she wore a small gold bead on a cord around her neck. A bead that looked just like the beads on my bracelet. It was even glowing.

"Do you know how to get it off?" I asked, breathless.

Her brow creased. "Isn't there a clasp?"

"No," I said. I stuck out my wrist. "If you can get the bracelet off, you can have it."

She peered at the bracelet and tried to slide it off my wrist. "It's not budging," she said.

"I know."

"Hold on," she said, reaching into her black leather purse and taking out a pair of pliers.

"Do you always carry tools in your purse?" I asked.

"Only when I need to open a bracelet," she said, and tried to cut through the cord.

"Careful," I said.

She tried once, twice, three times. The pliers didn't work.

"It won't come off," she said, frowning.

"So I'm stuck with it forever?" I asked, my voice rising.

"I don't know what else to do," the woman said, shaking her head.

"I want it off!" I yelled, panicking.

"So do I!" she said, grimacing. "But I can't do it!"

The lights overhead started flickering.

What was happening? More magic?

No.

It was cake time. My mom had bought a huge rectangular cake at the grocery store. She had placed it on the kitchen table and was lighting the candles.

Mom glanced over at the blond woman and frowned. I could tell she was wondering who she was and why she was at the party.

"I better go," the woman said, noticing my mom's gaze.

Flustered, I waved my hand at her. "You're leaving me with this?"

"I'll find you some other time," the woman hissed.

"But . . . but . . ."

She put her pliers back in her purse and disappeared out the front door.

What was I going to do now? My heart was still racing. No one could get the bracelet off! Would the magic last forever?

If only I could wish the magic away. But how could I get more wishes?

That's when I realized. My birthday cake. Which meant . . . birthday *candles.*

Yes, yes, yes!

Of course. I could wish for the magic to end!

My mom brought the cake to where I stood in the living room. It had chocolate frosting and eleven candles: ten, plus one for good luck.

Everyone starting singing.

"Happy birthday to you, happy birthday to you, happy birthday, dear Becca, happy birthday to you!"

"What are you going to wish for?" Harper asked, standing beside me. Georgette was on the other side of her.

I knew exactly what I was going to wish for.

I closed my eyes.

I wished that the magic on the bracelet would end. That people would want to be my friend only when they liked me—not because they had to be.

I opened my eyes. Then I blew.

All the flames went out in one big whoosh.

"Yay, Becca!" everyone cheered.

"You're the best!"

"Are ya ONE, are ya TWO . . ."

The singing got louder and louder, and the cheers got louder.

Everyone was hugging me and wishing me a happy birthday.

No one was leaving.

I touched the bracelet. It was still warm. It was still glowing. It was *still* working. My wish hadn't worked at all.

My bracelet was a curse.

✳ 11 ✳

Please Leave

While everyone ate cake, I snuck into my room to get some alone time.

But of course there were tons of people in there, too. A bunch of kids were sprawled out on the floor. Two people were sitting on my desk chair. And three girls I didn't even know were jumping on my bed—with their shoes on!

"Happy birthday, Becca!" one of the jumping girls said.

"Please don't jump on my bed," I begged.

"Becca said to stop!" the girl yelled, yanking the other two girls' arms.

One of those girls fell forward, knocking into my desk chair, which sent the desk chair rolling . . . right into Twinkle's bowl.

Ahhh!

The bowl tilted over and smashed to my floor. Glass shards went everywhere.

Twinkle slid across the wood floor toward my bed like he was on a Slip 'N Slide.

"Twinkle!" I yelled.

"Who?"

"What happened?"

"You're the best, Becca!"

"Mom!" I yelled.

But it was so loud in the apartment she couldn't hear me.

I tried to lie down on the floor to find my fish, but there were people in the way.

"What happened?" Shep asked, running into my room.

"Can you get me a glass of water?" I asked him. Then I took a deep breath and yelled, "EVERYONE ELSE, OUT OF MY ROOM! PLEASE LEAVE! GOOD-BYE!"

Everyone stared at me.

"Where does she want us to go?"

"PLEASE JUST GO!" I yelled again. I could feel stress hives forming on my face and I didn't even care.

My room slowly cleared out.

I got on my belly, trying to spot Twinkle under my bed.

And finally there he was!

His little body was flailing back and forth.

Poor Twinkle!

I gently picked him up with one hand and used my other palm to help shimmy out from under the bed.

Shep was already there with a glass of water. "Here you go. Poor betta."

I dropped Twinkle inside the glass of water. He fluttered around for a bit. He was dazed and sluggish. Would he be okay? He had to be okay.

"You're bleeding," Shep said to me, pointing to my arm.

Oh. I was. I had shimmied over a small glass shard. I looked around my room and saw that there were glass remnants from the fishbowl everywhere.

The noise in the living room was almost unbearable.

I needed to clean up my arm. I needed to clean up my living room.

I needed everyone to leave my house.

"Do you want me to tell everyone the party's over?" Shep asked.

My eyes filled with tears. I nodded. "Thank you," I whispered.

Shep got up and closed my door behind him.

"Party's over, everyone! Please call your parents and tell them it's time to come get you!" I heard him announce.

I sat silently, leaning against my bed and holding Twinkle in the glass.

My door opened. "Becca?" It was Harper. "Do you still want me to sleep over?" she asked, biting her thumbnail.

"I'm not feeling great," I told her. "So maybe another time?"

"Of course," she said. Was that relief on her face? "Feel better! Happy birthday!"

She closed the door behind her. I heard her say, "Georgette, I can sleep at your place and then we can go to the tournament together!"

Deep breath. Deep breath.

I continued taking deep breaths until the apartment quieted.

When it sounded like everyone had left, I got up and placed Twinkle's glass carefully on my dresser. He seemed fine now, swimming around. I exhaled. I'd just have to get him a new bowl.

I glared at the bracelet. Why wouldn't it come off?

I took a pair of scissors from my drawer and tried to squeeze through the beads to cut the cord.

Nothing.

My mom came into my room.

"You all right, sweetheart?"

I shook my head. I showed her the blood on my arm.

"Let me help," she said.

"Do you see any way to get this bracelet off?" I asked.

She took my hand in hers and squinted at it. "Is there no clasp?"

I shook my head.

"Let me get scissors."

"I tried that," I said, and sighed.

"We can take it to a jewelry store," she said.

"Okay," I said. But I was becoming convinced that it was never ever coming off.

Was there a trick? Was it a test? Had I failed?

My mom gave me an antihistamine for my hives. Then she washed my cut and put a Band-Aid on.

"You go to sleep," my mom said to me. "I'll clean up."

I shook my head. "I'll do it."

"No way. We'll clean together," she said.

"I'll help, too," Brahm said. "Raging party, Becca."

"Yeah," I said.

So we cleaned together. My brother put some music back on, and the three of us carefully picked up the glass, collected the garbage, wiped off the surfaces, swept the wood floors, and vacuumed the carpet.

Brahm and I brought all the garbage downstairs to the bins that were just off the lobby.

Mr. Wangins was sorting the recycling. Doodles was on his shoulder.

"Ahoy, Brahm!" Mr. Wangins said. "Ahoy, Becca! I hear it was your birthday! How was it?"

"Bad birthday, bad Becca!" Doodles squawked before I could answer. Then she added, "Hi, Brahm! Love you, Brahm!"

I turned to my brother, surprised. "Doodles loves you? Why does she love you?"

And do all parrots talk this much?

Brahm stepped up close to the parrot and made a kissy face. "Hi, Doodles," he said. "How are you?" He petted Doodles's back, and Doodles ruffled her feathers happily.

I laughed in shock.

Brahm and I said good night to Mr. Wangins and headed back through the lobby toward the elevator.

"What's your trick with Doodles?" I asked Brahm.

"I sing to her," my brother said. "I pet her, too. And sometimes I give her treats when she comes to my window."

"She comes to mine, too!"

"And what do you do?"

"I ignore her? Or I tell her to go away."

"Well, why would she be nice to you if you're not nice to her?"

"Oh," I said.

My brother shrugged.

We reached the elevator, and I pressed the button to call it down to the lobby.

"Hey, Brahm? How do you have so many friends?" I asked him.

"Are you kidding?" He laughed. "Did you not just experience your party? You have way more friends than I do!"

"Today I did . . . Yeah. But in general. What do you do to make friends?"

He raised one eyebrow. "Sing to them and give them treats?"

I laughed. "I'm serious."

"I don't know. I text people a lot. I hang out with people a lot."

"But how do you get them to hang out with you?"

"I ask them to," he said. The elevator finally came, and Brahm pulled open the door. "And I try to make sure they're having fun while we're hanging out. Like, I'll offer to play cards if I know they like cards." He smiled at me.

"But do you like cards?" I asked.

"Yeah."

"But what if they like something you don't?" I asked as we got on the elevator. I pressed the button for seven.

"I try to find something we both like."

I thought of Harper. "What if there's nothing?"

"If we have nothing in common, maybe we shouldn't be friends. You don't need to be friends with everyone. But everyone has something in common, yeah? Even if it's just that, I don't know, you both like pizza."

"Everyone likes pizza," I said. If only making friends came more naturally to me.

Then I wondered: If making friends was so easy for my brother, why was he usually such a jerk to me?

"Hey, Brahm?" I added as the elevator reached our floor. "Why are you always mean to me? Not this week, but normally?"

"I am?"

I nodded, tears pricking my eyes.

He blushed. "I don't know. Maybe because you're always around? I have to be cranky to someone and you can't get rid of me, so . . ."

"I like it better when you're nice," I said softly.

"I'll try to be nice, then," he said, and squeezed my shoulder.

I patted his hand. "Thanks."

When we got back to our apartment, I was exhausted. All I wanted to do was sleep for a week.

I took a shower, not bothering to protect my bracelet. Maybe the magic *would* wash off. I put on my pajamas. I checked on Twinkle. He was still doing okay in his tall glass of water.

"Sorry, Twinkle," I said. "I'll take better care of you, I promise."

I checked my phone. I had fifty more texts.

Elijah: Awesome party!

Elizabeth: Quiz: What your birth time says about you!

Emma: I was born at 11 p.m.! That means I'm a party animal!

Daisy: 🎉 Thank you for a fun night!

Zuri: 🎉 Happy birthday!

Willow: Thank you for inviting me! Hope the rest of the party was great!

Unknown Number: Happy birthday, Becca! Here is a picture of me at my tenth birthday! Look at those bangs LOL. XO Ms. Michaels.

Shep: How is Twinkle?

Nothing from Harper and Georgette. I guessed they were busy having a sleepover. And watering plants.

I had three hundred more friend requests on Friendstagram. Mostly from people I didn't know.

My father still hadn't called.

I turned off my phone, got into bed, and went to sleep.

✳ 12 ✳

The Day After

When I woke up the next day, I felt like there was a heavy weight on my chest.

I stared at my arm. The bracelet was still on. Was I ever going to be able to take it off?

Was I ever going to be able to live normally?

I turned on my phone. There were a hundred new texts and a voice mail from my dad. He'd called at 11:35 p.m.

"Sorry I missed you, honey! I meant to call earlier. I guess you're asleep. Happy birthday! I hope it was a great day. I owe you a present. Tell me what you want!"

What did I want? I wanted him to remember my birthday.

"Bad birthday! Bad birthday!" I heard a voice squawk outside.

Doodles was perched on the sill outside my window.

I thought about what my brother had said. Instead of ignoring Doodles, I opened the window.

"Bad Becca!"

I put out my arm. "Hello there," I said softly. "Come here."

Doodles cocked her head to one side but did step closer.

I reached out a hand and very carefully stroked her feathers.

"Do you like that, Doodles?" I asked the parrot.

"Hello there," Doodles squawked, stepping onto my hand. Her claws tickled, and I laughed.

"Hello," I said.

Was that all it took? All I'd had to do was open the window?

Doodled pecked at my bracelet with her beak.

"Can you get it off?" I asked. "That would be helpful. I can't get the magic to stop."

She pecked at it again. "Helpful. Helpful!"

Then Doodles glanced up and noticed Twinkle in his glass of water.

"Doodles, meet Twinkle. Twinkle, meet Doodles," I said. "Doodles, promise me you won't eat Twinkle, 'kay? He had a rough night."

"Doodles eat Twinkle, yes."

"No, Doodles, I said don't eat Twinkle. Please."

"Don't eat Twinkles," Doodles said. She jumped off my arm and flew back out the window. "Helpful!"

I wasn't sure not eating Twinkle was helping exactly, but it wasn't *not* helping.

I closed the window and went into the living room. Mom and Brahm were still asleep. The apartment was quiet and clean, but the wall by the window was piled with presents.

So many colorful boxes.

I plucked out the present from Harper first.

The card said:

Happy birthday, bestie!
Love, Harper

Then I opened the box. It was a plant.

I laughed to myself. It was pretty—of course it was. And it was nice of her to get me something at all. But she was the one who was into plants.

I opened Georgette's box next.

Another plant.

I probably should have opened these last night.

I opened more boxes. The Three Es had given me a

purple tiara. Zuri, Corinne, and Daisy had gotten me a sweater that was too big.

All these people had bought me something, which was so generous of them, but none of them knew much about me. Or even what size I was.

I spotted the small, rectangular box that Willow had brought.

I unwrapped it carefully and saw two things inside.

A book called *Dragon Night #1*.

And a blank red notebook.

Then I read her card:

Hi Becca,

Here's a fantasy series you might like! I loved it. And a blank book so you can write something new.

XO
Willow

Instead of opening the rest of the presents, I climbed back into bed and started reading *Dragon Night #1*.

As I read about prophecies and dragons, I drowned out everything around me. The texts coming in on my phone, Mom and Brahm in the kitchen, even the city sounds of honking outside. All I could think about was the story. Before I knew it, I had read the whole thing.

"Mom?" I asked after I was done. "Can we go get the next book in this series?"

My mom and I walked into Books in Wonderland. It's a small, bright bookstore on 85th Street. The shelves are over-flowing with hardcovers and paperbacks, picture books and board books. On the wall in the back, there are first editions in a glass case.

Guess who was in the bookstore.

Guess!

Yes! Willow!

"Hi!" I said, running up to her.

"Isn't this place the best?" she asked.

I nodded. I couldn't believe she was here, too. It felt like . . . magic.

"Sorry I snuck out last night," she said. "I get weird when there are too many people."

"Me too," I said, laughing. "Thank you for the book. I loved it."

"You read it already?" she squealed.

"Yes!"

"Did you like the part when the wizard turns out to be . . . wait, no, that's book two. I'm not telling you!"

"I'm getting book two right now!"

"Yay!"

She brought me straight to the Dragon Night section of the store and pulled out books two and three. "There's also a graphic novel," she said. "And an activity book! And I heard there's going to be a movie, but the movie—"

"Is never as good as the book," I finished.

"Exactly."

We pored over all the books, laughing and dissecting the cover art until our mothers joined us.

"Do you and your mom always dress the same?" Willow whispered, eyeing our matching black leggings and yellow sweaters.

"Don't ask," I told her.

"We were just talking about getting coffee and going to sit in the park for a bit," Willow's mom said. "Sound good?"

Willow and I both nodded. It sounded great.

The weather was perfect: one of those crisp fall days when the leaves in Central Park are starting to turn yellow and orange. Everyone was outside, walking dogs and pushing strollers. Willow and I sat on one bench, and our mothers sat on another one beside us.

"I'm so glad I ran into you in the library during capture the flag," Willow told me. "I know you have a million friends and everything, but I always thought you seemed nice. I remember telling my parents that last year."

I had forgotten that Willow was in my class in fourth grade. She had moved to our school from downtown in September.

I flushed as I thought about how she was always on her own, reading. I had been so focused on Harper, I hadn't tried to befriend anyone else. Even the new girl who didn't know anyone.

I should have reached out. I should have opened a window. Maybe I still could.

"Want to hang out after school one day?" I asked Willow.

Willow nodded. "Maybe we could get bubble tea on Wednesday," she said. "I am obsessed with bubble tea, but only the black tapioca and not the white because it looks like snot, you know? Oh, I'm sorry if you like the white—I didn't mean to yuck your yum. I won't judge you if you get white, really. Well, maybe a little bit."

I laughed. "I will try any kind of bubble tea."

"Do you like making earrings, by any chance? I just got

this kit, and I've been making a ton of them. We could also do that."

"Yes!" I said, touching my small earrings. "I only have the studs that I got mine pierced with."

"Then we'll make earrings!"

"Yay! Wait, did you make those ones that look like tiny pizzas? I am obsessed with pizza."

"Yes! I did! And I love your bracelet, by the way. It's so unusual."

Right. My bracelet. That's why Willow had asked me about bubble tea and making earrings. Not because she really wanted to be my friend. She was just under the spell.

The bracelet was warm. It was always warm. It was always glowing. It was always working. Even this—my friendship with Willow—wasn't real.

"I can't get it off," I told her. "It's stuck."

"Really?"

"Yeah. I've tried everything."

"Want me to try?" she asked.

"Sure," I said. "But I don't think it will help."

I put out my arm. She touched the bracelet and studied it. "I think this is the clasp, yeah?"

"There's no clasp . . ." I said, but she was already fiddling with it.

"No, there is. I see it," she said. "Right here. I can open it. Just give me a second . . ."

"Okay," I said, my heart thumping. Where had that clasp come from? "But listen. If this works—which it probably won't—you might not want to hang out with me anymore."

She laughed. "Why not?"

"I'm just saying it's a possibility."

"That's bananas," she said, and the next thing I knew, she'd opened the clasp.

The bracelet was in her hand. It was off!

"Here you go," Willow said, handing it to me with a smile.

The bracelet was off. I couldn't believe it. Tingles ran over my body. A gust of wind blew over me. Something had changed. I knew it. The spell was done. The bracelet was cool in my hand and it was no longer glowing.

"I'm free!" I squealed.

Willow blinked twice and stared at me again. She shook her head.

"It's okay if you want to cancel Wednesday," I said. "I won't be upset. I mean, I will be, but I understand."

She tilted her head to the side. "Why would I cancel?"

"If you don't want to hang out anymore."

"Why wouldn't I want to hang out anymore?" She laughed. "I honestly have no idea what you're talking about."

"Because . . . because . . . people change their minds. About friends." My eyes filled with tears. I thought of Harper. I thought of my parents. "People change their minds all the time."

"Totally true," Willow said, hugging her knees. "I did not want to leave Tribeca at all. Have you been to Pier 25? With the mini putt? It's amazing. It's a block from my old apartment. And two of my friends lived in my building. Two! But then my parents wanted to be closer to work, so we moved uptown. I cried for a week. I miss my friends. I miss the pier. But now I have Central Park and the best bookstore nearby, so yeah, things change, but change isn't always bad. And I can't wait for Wednesday."

I suddenly felt lighter. She was right. Things changed, people changed, but new could be good.

I glanced over at my mom. She was laughing with Willow's mom.

I hadn't seen her laugh with a friend in a long time. Maybe she was changing, too.

I smiled to myself.

Then I paused.

Why had Willow been able to remove the bracelet? What had changed?

Oh.

It was all of a sudden really obvious. Something *had* changed. Something big. I had made a friend.

Maybe that's what the magic was all about. I had wished that everybody wanted to be my friend. But what I'd really needed was to learn how to make a friend. How to open a window and connect—really connect—with someone new. And I'd finally done it.

"You got it off!" I heard someone say. I looked up to see the fancy blond woman standing on the path in front of our bench. She was wearing a beige cashmere coat, and her eyes were gleaming. "Well done. Can I have it now?"

I jumped, startled to see her there.

Willow gawked at the woman. "Do you know her?" she asked me.

"Not exactly."

"I want that bracelet," the woman said firmly. "And I'll give you fifty dollars for it. No, one hundred dollars for it."

"I . . ."

"You're done with it! You don't need it! And I do!" the woman snapped, her face getting stern. "You said I could have it!"

I had said that, but that was when it was stuck. And this woman really creeped me out. How had she found me? What would she do with the magic?

"Two hundred dollars," she said.

"Um . . ." Two hundred dollars is a lot of money. A lot. But hadn't the note said I should "keep the box to mail the magic off" or something like that?

"I don't understand what's happening," Willow said nervously. "Should I get your mom?"

"You're going to give me that bracelet," the blond woman said. "Now. Got it?"

"No, I'm not," I said.

And then the woman reached over and knocked my hand, sending the bracelet flying into the air.

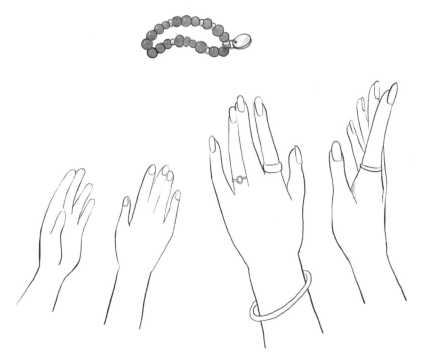

"Ouch!" I yelled.

The woman grabbed the bracelet off the ground and ran.

"Did that person just steal your bracelet?" Willow asked, incredulous.

"Yes! We need to stop her!" I cried.

Willow and I jumped up off the bench and started to run through Central Park after the woman.

"Becca!" my mom screamed behind us. "Where are you going? Stop!"

"Willow!" Willow's mom yelled. "Come back!"

I heard dogs barking and babies crying but I didn't stop. I kept running. Willow was just a few paces behind me.

The woman was getting away. She'd knocked my hand and stolen the bracelet! She was not a good person! What kind of wish would she make with the magic? It could be terrible!

The woman ran faster, and the space between us was growing. Up ahead, I saw her veer off the path and into a grassy area.

"Somebody heeeeeeelp!" I cried. But the woman was gone. And the magic was gone with her.

∗ 13 ∗

Step Away

"Becca! Willow! What are you doing? Don't move another muscle!" my mom shouted.

I stopped and turned around to see my mom and Willow's mom huffing and puffing behind us.

"But that woman stole my bracelet!" I explained between pants.

"Yeah!" Willow said. "I saw it happen."

"That doesn't mean you should run after her!" my mom replied. Her cheeks were bright red and her hands were on her hips.

"She could be dangerous!" Willow's mom added.

"But—"

Suddenly I heard a shriek from somewhere up ahead.

"Hey!" a woman's voice cried out. "Drop it! Come back!"

I exchanged a glance with Willow. Had the blond woman stolen from someone else?

I knew Mom would be angry but I couldn't help it. I ran off the path and into the grassy area where the woman had run. I could hear Willow, my mom, and Willow's mom following close behind me.

There, at the base of a big tree, a person was sprawled on the ground.

"Are you okay?" I asked, breathless and worried.

"No, I am not okay!" the woman yelled back, standing up and glaring at me.

It was the creepy blond woman!

I took a step toward her. "Give me back my bracelet!"

"I couldn't even if I wanted to," she sneered. "That horrid creature appeared out of nowhere and stole it!"

"What creature?" I asked, looking around. "A dog? Did a dog take my bracelet?" I didn't see a dog anywhere around us. We had somehow stumbled into an empty area of the park.

"Becca! We're getting out of here," my mother said, appearing beside me and gripping my shoulder. Willow and her mom were right behind us.

The blond woman raised her arms to the sky, talking more to herself than to me. "I was so close!" she cried. "I had it in my hands! And now it's gone!"

My mother quickly snapped a photo of the woman on her phone, and then pulled me in the other direction. "Becca, I'm sorry about your bracelet, but we're getting out of here immediately."

"But, Mom—"

"Immediately."

Before I could say another word, my mom and Willow's mom had hustled me and Willow away from the blond woman and out of Central Park.

Once we were back in our apartment, Mom hugged me a million times, even though she was furious at me for chasing the blond woman. "Don't you know how dangerous that could have been? It's just a bracelet. Let it go!"

"I'm sorry," I told her. But I couldn't stop thinking about it. How had the blond woman found me? What kind of creature had taken the bracelet? Where was the bracelet now?

As punishment, my mom disabled my Friendstagram account.

"I don't think you should have one anyway," she said. "I've been thinking about it, and it's a bad idea. I'm also not sure about the iPhone."

"Please don't take the phone, too," I begged. "It's easier for me to be in touch with Dad with it."

She hesitated. "Fine. But I'm going to limit your screen time."

I sighed. Mom was back to being a parent, not my friend. Which was annoying in some ways, but in other ways, it was a relief.

It was nice to have my mom be my mom.

I thought about my dad. I hadn't responded to his birthday text. He had sent me a follow-up one this morning. I hadn't responded to that, either.

I suddenly realized why.

I was mad. I was *really* mad at him.

But I couldn't stew forever. Maybe it was time to reach out.

I went into my room, closed the door, and called him.

His voice mail picked up. I was about to leave a message when he sent me a text. Yup. Another text.

Dad: Hi honey! Did you have a good birthday? I'm just catching up on some work. Can I call you later?

I hesitated but then typed back:

Me: Dad, I'm mad at you. You forgot my birthday! I call and text all the time, and you're never there!

I know you're busy with work, but I'm still your kid and I should be a priority!

I sent the text and held my breath. I had never said those things to my dad before. I didn't know how he would react.

My phone rang in my hand, startling me. It was my dad.

"Hi," I said softly.

"Hi, Becca," he said. "I . . . I am so sorry. So sorry."

I stayed quiet.

"I miss you so much," he said.

"Then why don't you call me back?" I whispered, my throat tight.

"I love hearing your voice. But I think . . . I think it also makes me sad. Because I miss you. I hate living so far from you. But that is no excuse for not being there for you. I promise to call more often."

"Okay." I swallowed. "Like how often? Twice a week?"

"At least."

"Three times a week, then."

"Three times a week," he repeated. "And I owe you a birthday present. Like, a really big one."

"I don't need any more presents," I told him. "I just need your presence. Your presence is my present."

He laughed. "Isn't there something else you'd want?"

My arm suddenly felt very bare. "Oh. How about a bracelet? Can you choose one you like?" It wouldn't be magical, but it would be from my dad. Something he picked out just for me.

"Definitely," he said. "And I think I'll fly in a few days before Brahm's bar mitzvah. So we can have some extra time together."

"Yes," I said. "That."

"Come on, everyone, dinner!" my mother called out.

"Dad? I gotta go. Dinner."

"Tofu? Salmon?"

"Probably one of those," I said, and giggled.

"I love you," he said.

"I love you, too."

"Happy birthday, Becca."

I hung up the phone, feeling better than I had in a long time. I went to the kitchen, where Brahm was pouring himself a glass of water and Mom was heating up food.

"Can't we have pizza again?" Brahm was asking Mom.

"No," my mom said, shaking her head. "We've had enough pizza to last us until Becca's next birthday. We're having salmon."

Ha. I sat down at the table.

"Can you pour me a glass of water?" I asked Brahm, since he was still standing.

"Pour it yourself," he replied.

"Brahm!" Mom chided him. "Get your sister water!"

My brother huffed and banged a glass of water in front of me.

"Thanks," I said.

"Becca, are you going to open the rest of the presents?" Mom asked, gesturing toward the living room with its stacks of gifts. "Where are we going to put all that stuff?"

I'd had an idea on our walk back from the park today. "I was thinking of donating the gifts," I said. "To Goodwill. There's a sign in the window about donations."

My mom nodded. "That would be lovely. You can keep a couple of favorites and donate the rest. You should still send thank-you notes to everyone who brought you something, though."

"I will," I said. That was going to take forever.

"You should write the thank-you notes after dinner. After you and Brahm do the dishes," Mom added.

"You should do my share of the dishes since I got you the water," my brother said.

I sighed.

Yup. The magic was long gone.

✳ 14 ✳

What Happens Next

On Monday morning, the temperature dropped and everyone was wearing jackets. I spotted Harper by herself in the schoolyard. I took a deep breath and approached her.

"So how was the chess tournament?" I asked.

"Georgette came in first. I didn't place, but I won two out of my five games," she said.

"That's still great," I said. "Congrats!"

"Are you feeling better?" she asked. "You seemed pretty upset on your birthday."

"I was. I'm better now. I guess I just . . ." I hesitated.

"Yeah?"

I stood there for a minute. "I understand what you were saying last Monday." I couldn't believe it had been only a week ago. "When you said you didn't think we were best friends anymore."

"You do?"

"You're closer with Georgette now. You *both* like chess. And Friendstagram. And plants. Thanks for the plant, by the way."

"You're welcome."

"My point is, we used to do everything together, but you were right. Or your mom was right. It's okay if we go different ways. People change. We both changed."

Harper looked relieved. "Yeah?"

"Yeah. But that doesn't mean we can't talk anymore. We can still be regular friends, even if we're not best friends, don't you think?"

Harper smiled big. "Yes! For sure!"

"Okay. Good."

I saw her look across the yard and wave to Georgette, who ran over.

"OMG, I have to show you something on Friendstagram," Georgette said to Harper.

I waved good-bye to them and turned away.

One benefit of not being best friends with Harper anymore? I didn't have to spend time with Georgette.

I spotted the Three Es in the yard and approached them cautiously. Would they ignore me? Want nothing to do with me?

The three of them were in formation, trying out a complicated dance move.

"What's up?" I asked.

"Becca!" Elijah said. "You didn't respond to any texts yesterday! And you didn't like any of our posts."

"Or do any of my quizzes," Elizabeth said.

"What's up with you?" Emma asked, crossing her arms.

"I'm sorry," I said. "Yesterday was busy."

"Day-after-birthday blues?" Emma asked.

"Kind of," I said.

"Well, we don't like being ghosted," Elijah said. "Not cool."

"You're right," I said. "I should have texted. And I should have thanked you for the awesome tiara. It's very sparkly."

"We thought it was so you," Emma said.

"Are you going to watch that video I sent?" Elijah asked. "I want us to know the dance by Friday, latest. We have to practice at lunch. Becca, are you in?"

I liked them a lot. But I didn't want to be the fourth E. "I think I might sit this one out. I totally appreciate you inviting me, though. And I would like to formally request a front-row seat to any performances," I said.

"Oh! Okay. Sure," Emma said.

"We'll miss you," Elijah said. "But this dance number would work better for a trio. So it's not the worst thing."

"Sounds good. See you in class," I said, waving.

I got into line and waited until Principal Bort nodded at me.

"Morning, Mort," I said.

He pursed his lips. "I think it's best if you call me Principal Bort."

I blushed. "Of course. Sorry."

"But I'm glad you like the scarf," he said, noticing I was wearing it.

I did like the scarf. It was zigzaggy. But really soft.

"Wear it well," he said.

I walked upstairs and into my classroom. It was odd—no one cheered. I sat at my desk in the front.

I stared at Willow's empty seat.

Where was she? What if she was sick? What if she'd moved back downtown? What if she didn't want to be friends after all?

I looked around the room. I tried to wave to Shep, but he was focused on whatever he was drawing.

"Everyone please hand in your homework," Ms. Michaels said.

Oops.

I'd totally forgotten about my homework.

I cringed. "I'm so sorry. I forgot to do it."

Ms. Michaels sighed. "Becca, Becca, Becca. What am I going to *do* with you?"

I cracked a smile. "Let me bring it in tomorrow?"

Her face stayed stern. But then she cracked a smile, too. "Just this once. I'm in a good mood today." She lowered her voice, leaned over to me, and said, "I auditioned for a role in a new show yesterday. *101 Dalmatians*. Thank you for inviting me to sing on Friday—it reminded me how much I love it."

"Hurrah!" I cheered, jumping up.

"Sit," she said sternly. "Now, everyone *please* take out your spelling books."

My A-plus days just for being me were over.

I would have to try harder. I could be hardworking. And responsible. And meticulous! Even if I'm still not sure how to spell *meticulous*.

I will learn.

At lunchtime, I was walking to the cafeteria when I heard:

"Becca! Becca, wait up!"

Willow jogged up next to me.

"You're here! Finally! Where were you?" I asked.

"Doctor's appointment. You okay? What's wrong?"

I threw my arms around her. "I am just glad to see you.

And I wanted to know if you wanted to . . . wanted to . . . sit together at lunch," I managed to say nervously.

Willow grinned. "Yeah. Are you gonna get the hot lunch, or do you bring from home?"

"My mom packed me tofu and broccoli," I said.

"That sounds . . . healthy."

"It is. Was your mom freaked out about the woman in the park yesterday?" I asked Willow.

"Totally. Your mom sent her picture to park security, yeah?"

I nodded. "But it was pretty blurry."

"You were so brave!" Willow added, hand on her heart. "Running after her!"

"You ran, too," I said.

"I ran after you," she said. "My mom was mad at me for that. But she had a great time talking to your mom. I think they've been texting!"

"No way!" My mom didn't have too many friends. I was glad she was trying to make a new one. Someone who wasn't me. I liked her better as a mom than a friend.

Willow and I headed into the cafeteria together.

"Where do you want to sit?" she asked.

I pointed to Shep in the corner. He was sitting with Zuri and Daisy, showing them how to draw something. "With them?"

"Sure." She smiled.

I was glad Shep had new friends, too. Maybe it was because of what I had done at the assembly? I looked around the cafeteria. Sure, I didn't have my bracelet anymore, but there were other ways to help people.

Another girl in our grade named Talia was sitting alone. I didn't know why she was alone. Maybe her best friend had dumped her, too. Maybe she was shy. Maybe she *wanted* to sit alone. Who knew? It didn't hurt to reach out, did it?

"Hey, Talia," I said, approaching her. "We're going to sit over there with Shep if you want to join our table."

Her eyes widened in surprise. "Oh! Thanks. Yeah. That would be great. I usually sit with Jeremy, but he's sick today . . ."

So we all joined Shep, Daisy, and Zuri.

Maybe I didn't have magic on my arm anymore. But maybe it didn't matter.

Maybe the bracelet had taught me to make my own magic.

"Becca!" my brother yelled.

"What?" I yelled back.

I was in my room finishing my homework and carefully putting it in my bag. I was not forgetting again.

"Right, Twinkle?" I said. "You won't let me forget?" Luckily, Twinkle had made a full recovery.

"Are you coming?" my brother called from the hallway.

"To do what?"

"To play Rummy!"

I opened my door to see Brahm standing there. "Really?"

"Yeah," he said with a shrug.

"Really truly? You still want to play with me?" I asked.

"You told me to be nicer, so I'm being nicer! What's your problem?"

I smiled. "No problem. I'm in."

"I'm playing, too!" my mom called out from the kitchen.

"Family game night!" I cheered.

"I'll make popcorn," my brother said, and we headed into the kitchen.

Suddenly the front doorbell rang.

My mom looked through the peephole. "It's Mr. Wangins. Hello there!" she said, opening the door.

"Ahoy! How is everyone this evening?" Mr. Wangins asked. Doodle was on his shoulder.

"We're fine. Is everything okay?" Mom asked the super.

"Doodles is looking for Becca," he said. "She keeps repeating her name."

"Becca! Stop her! Please!" Doodles squawked.

"Does she hate me again?" I asked, taking a step back.

"No, no, she got something for you," Mr. Wangins said. "Here you go."

And he handed me the bracelet.

The magic bracelet!

My jaw dropped. What? Why? How?

"Stop her!" Doodles squawked again. "Stop her! Helpful!"

"How did she get this?" I asked, delighted and completely confused.

"Yesterday afternoon," Mr. Wangins explained, "I let Doodles out to fly around the courtyard, but instead she flew straight to Central Park! She's never done that before. And when she got back, she had this bracelet in her beak. And she's been saying 'Stop her!' and 'Becca' and 'Helpful' over and over again. So now I'm wondering if this bracelet belongs to you?"

I was amazed. "It does," I said, trying to understand.

The blond lady had yelled about a creature appearing out of nowhere and stealing the bracelet.

Had she meant a bird?

Had she meant *this* bird?

I looked right at Doodles.

"You heard me calling for help and flew over to steal back my bracelet?" I asked incredulously.

"Doodles helpful," Doodles said.

"Thank you, Doodles, you're amazing." I reached over and caressed the feathers around her head. "Good bird. Such a good bird!"

"That's your bracelet?" my mom asked me. "The one the woman grabbed at the park?"

I nodded.

"Unbelievable," my mom said.

"That is one special bird," Brahm added.

And one special bracelet.

"Thank you so much," I said to Mr. Wangins. "It was really nice of you to bring it here tonight." Mr. Wangins was always nice. Before the bracelet, during the bracelet, and after.

"Ahoy!" he said, heading for the door.

"Wait! Mr. Wangins?" I asked. "Can we offer you a piece of cake from my birthday?"

"Sure," he said.

I was suddenly embarrassed that I hadn't brought him a slice over the weekend.

I went to the fridge, cut him a piece, and put it on a plate wrapped in tinfoil. "Thank you again," I said. "And, Mr. Wangins?"

"Yes, Becca?"

I thought of all the times he'd asked me how I was. Had I ever returned the question? "Did you have a good day?" I asked.

He nodded, smiling. "I did! Thank you for asking!"

I smiled back.

I wondered if the most important part of friendship was showing that you cared.

I thought of Shep. And Harper. And Willow.

But friendship is also about being there when people need you. Seeing them for who they really are. And showing them who *you* really are.

"Good night, Mr. Wangins," I said as he left with Doodles. "Ahoy!"

"Bye, Becca!" Doodles squawked.

"I can't believe Doodles got that bracelet from the thief," my mom said, closing the front door and shaking her head. "Incredible."

I couldn't believe it, either. I went into my room, sat on my bed, and examined the bracelet in awe. I had it back!

It was no longer glowing, and the beads were cool in my hand. There was definitely a small gold circular clasp, which I swear had not been there before.

Now what had the letter said I was supposed to do with it?

I pulled the box out from under my bed and reread the note.

> Because you're blue,
> This bracelet is now for you.
> Speak one wish to make it true.
> (There are some things it cannot do.)
> Keep the box to mail the magic off
> When you are through.
> Take care and beware.
> Hugs and kisses,
> And best wishes.

Mail the magic off when I was through? But who was I supposed to send it to? Could I give it to Willow? To Shep? To anyone I wanted?

Did I want to try making another wish?

I shook my head. One wish had been more than enough, thank you very much.

I checked inside the box and inside the pouch to see if there were any more instructions. Hmm. There weren't. Was I supposed to put the bracelet back inside the box and pass it on to anyone I felt like?

Even though the box said my name on the front?

Wait a minute. I did a double take at the box. It didn't say *my* name anymore.

Instead, in black fancy writing, it now said:

Addie Asante
6788 Kildare Street
Columbus, Ohio 43219

Oh! The name had changed! And I was supposed to send the box to a person named Addie! Addie Asante! She was getting the bracelet next!

Who was she? I had no idea. Was she just another kid like me? Had she had a really bad day? A bad week? A bad month? Was this Addie Asante feeling sad—feeling blue— right now?

Who'd had the box before me? Had my name and

address appeared on the package after another person was *through* with the magic?

And what about the blond woman? Who was she? Where was she? Did she know that I had the bracelet back and that I was supposed to mail it to Ohio?

I took a deep breath. The bracelet was magic, for sure, but it hadn't *all* been amazing. What if I sent the package off to this Addie and her wish made things worse for her?

Should I warn her about what could happen?

Could I follow the letter's instructions but still give her a heads-up?

I thought of the notebook Willow had given me.

So you can write something new, she'd said.

Oh. Yes. I *could* write something new.

"Becca! Popcorn's ready!" my brother yelled.

At the same time, my phone rang and my father's face popped up on-screen.

First, I was going to say hi to my dad.

Second, I was going to play cards.

But then I would write.

After the game, I took out the red notebook and wrote down everything that happened. I even drew some pictures. I'm no Shep, but I figured, why not? I put the bracelet back in the pouch, and then put the pouch and the old-looking letter back in the box.

And when I am done writing, I'm going to put this notebook inside the box, too. So you'll have a little more info than I did, Addie. About the bracelet. About the magic. About the creepy blond lady. (I hope she doesn't come after you, too!)

Then I'm going to bring the box to the post office.

And then . . .

Well, I don't know what happens then! I'm going to hope that this package gets all the way to Addie Asante, of Columbus, Ohio. All the way to YOU.

Maybe you're feeling lonely, too. Maybe you lost a friend. Or your dad moved away? Or maybe you're feeling blue about something else entirely.

I don't know why your name is on this box. But I hope you get it. And I hope you'll reach out to me when you do. I'm not on Friendstagram (anymore), but my email and phone number are on the back of this notebook. I'm here to talk about anything. I would love to hear from you.

Good luck, Addie. And best wishes.

XO Becca

READ ADDIE'S STORY IN

BEST WISHES #2: The Sister Switch

WRITTEN BY

SARAH MLYNOWSKI

AND

DEBBIE RIGAUD

COMING SOON

Acknowledgments

Thank you to all the publishing people for working their magic on this book:

Especially Aimee Friedman, who edited this book about a hundred times, and Laura Dail, my forever agent, who has been cheering this series on for over a hundred years. Thank you both for your never-ending support and trust.

More thank-yous to everyone at LDLA and Scholastic, especially Carrie Pestritto, Rachel Feld ♥, Taylan Salvati, Victoria Velez, Lauren Donovan, Erin Berger, Elizabeth Parisi, Olivia Valcarce, Arianna Arroyo, Lisa Sandell, Melissa Schirmer, Abby McAden, David Levithan, Ellie Berger, Lizette Serrano, Emily Heddleson, Alan Smagler, Elizabeth Whiting, and everyone in Sales and in the School

Channels. Thank you Natalie Lloyd and Mallory Kass for your insight and suggestions.

Thank you to Maxine Vee for the gorgeous cover and beautiful art.

Thanks to Austin Denesuk, Matthew Snyder, and Berni Barta at CAA.

Thanks to the amazing Lauren Walters.

Thank you, Brittany Schoellkopf! So grateful for all your help.

I wish every writer had writer friends as magical as I do. A million thanks to:

Emily Jenkins, for reading a very early draft and kicking my tush.

Courtney Sheinmel, for her careful read and constant cheerleading.

Stu Gibbs for talking me through the plot again and again.

Max Brallier for telling me THERE WERE TOO MANY THINGS and for understanding why I refused to add a tiny funny genie.

Morgan Matson for fixing all the problems.

Christina Soontornvat for her brilliant suggestions.

Adele Griffin for hosting and feeding me cheese platters, pie, and friendship.

Margot Miller for reading the book so quickly and giving me great notes! (And for having the world's best aunt.)

To the rest of my coworkers in crime: Julie Buxbaum, Rose Brock, Alan Gratz, Anne Heltzel, Karina Yan Glaser, Julia DeVillers, Elizabeth Eulberg, Gordon Korman, Leslie Margolis, Lauren Myracle, James Ponti, Melissa Posten, Debbie Rigaud, Rebecca Serle, Jennifer E. Smith, and Bob—thank you for judging covers, brainstorming titles, Zooming, texting, and making me laugh while I write. I appreciate you all.

Books in Wonderland was inspired by the amazing Books of Wonder in New York City. While it currently doesn't have a location on the Upper West Side, hopefully one day it will again.

Additional thanks and love to: Bonnie Altro, Elissa Ambrose & Robert Ambrose, the Bekers, Brett Berkowitz, Linda Guerrero & Ben Berkowitz (thank you for the name suggestion, Ben!), the Bilermans, Jess Braun, Rose Brock, Jeremy Cammy, the Deckers, Lauren Kisilevsky, the Mittlemans, Aviva Mlynowski, Larry Mlynowski & Louisa Weiss, Zibby Owens, Shobie Riff, and the Steins.

Love to my husband, Todd, and my daughters, Chloe and Anabelle. Thank you for your encouragement, snuggles, baked goods, BBQ, and inspiration. You are my wishes come true.

Read all the books in the Whatever After series!

Whatever After #1: FAIREST of ALL

In their first adventure, Abby and Jonah wind up in the story of Snow White. But when they stop Snow from eating the poisoned apple, they mess up the whole story! Can they still find Snow her happy ending?

Whatever After #2: IF the SHOE FITS

This time, Abby and Jonah find themselves in Cinderella's story. When Cinderella breaks her foot, the glass slipper won't fit! With a little bit of magic, quick thinking, and luck, can Abby and her brother save the day?

Whatever After #3: SINK or SWIM

Abby and Jonah are pulled into the tale of *The Little Mermaid* — a story with an ending that is *not* happy. So Abby and Jonah mess it up on purpose! Can they convince the mermaid to keep her tail before it's too late?

Whatever After #4: DREAM ON

Abby and Jonah are lost in Sleeping Beauty's story, along with Abby's friend Robin. Before they know it, Sleeping Beauty is wide awake and Robin is fast asleep. How will Abby and Jonah make things right?

Whatever After #5: BAD HAIR DAY

When Abby and Jonah fall into Rapunzel's story, they mess everything up by giving Rapunzel a haircut! Can they untangle this fairy tale disaster in time?

Whatever After #6: COLD as ICE

When their dog, Prince, runs through the mirror, Abby and Jonah have no choice but to follow him into the story of the Snow Queen. It's a winter wonderland . . . but the Snow Queen is mean, and she FREEZES Prince! Can Abby and Jonah save their dog . . . and themselves?

Whatever After #7: BEAUTY QUEEN

Abby and Jonah fall into the story of *Beauty and the Beast*. When Jonah is taken prisoner instead of Beauty, Abby has to find a way to fix this fairy tale . . . before things get pretty ugly!

Whatever After #8: ONCE upon a FROG

When Abby and Jonah fall into the story of *The Frog Prince*, they realize the princess is so rude they don't even *want* her help! But will they be able to figure out how to turn the frog back into a prince all by themselves?

Whatever After #9: GENIE in a BOTTLE

The mirror has dropped Abby and Jonah into the story of *Aladdin*! But when things go wrong with the genie, the siblings have to escape an enchanted cave, learn to fly a magic carpet, and figure out WHAT to wish for . . . so they can help Aladdin and get back home!

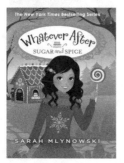

Whatever After #10: SUGAR and SPICE

When Abby and Jonah fall into *Hansel and Gretel*, they can't wait to see the witch's cake house (yum). But they didn't count on the witch trapping them there!

Whatever After #11: TWO PEAS in a POD

When Abby lands in *The Princess and the Pea*, everyone in the kingdom thinks SHE is the princess they've all been waiting for. Though Abby loves the royal treatment, she and Jonah need to find a real princess!

Whatever After #12: SEEING RED

When Abby and Jonah fall into *Little Red Riding Hood*, they're determined to save Little Red and her grandma from being eaten by the big, bad wolf. But there's quite a surprise in store at grandma's house.

Whatever After #13: SPILL the BEANS

Abby and Jonah FINALLY land in the story of *Jack and the Beanstalk*! But when they end up with the magic beans, can they get Jack out of his gigantic troubles?

Whatever After #14: GOOD as GOLD

In the story of *Goldilocks and the Three Bears*, there's porridge to sample and beds to test out! But if Abby and Jonah help Goldilocks, will they run into trouble with the Bear family?

Whatever After #15: JUST DANCE

Abby and Jonah land in the story of *The Twelve Dancing Princesses*. They'll have to learn some dance moves to get out of this magical mess in time!

Whatever After Special Edition #1: ABBY in WONDERLAND

In this Special Edition, Abby and three of her friends fall down a rabbit hole into *Alice's Adventures in Wonderland*! They meet the Mad Hatter, the caterpillar, and Alice herself . . . but only solving a riddle from the Cheshire Cat can help them escape the terrible Queen of Hearts. Includes magical games and an interview with the author!

Whatever After Special edition #2: ABBY in OZ

Abby and her friends are on a new adventure inside *The Wonderful Wizard of Oz*! Can they find the courage, brains, and heart to make it home? Includes a map of Oz and fun activities!

WHAT HAPPENS WHEN YOUR MAGIC GOES UPSIDE-DOWN?

From bestselling authors SARAH MLYNOWSKI, LAUREN MYRACLE, and EMILY JENKINS comes a series about finding your own kind of magic.

About the Author

SARAH MLYNOWSKI is the *New York Times* bestselling author of the Whatever After series, the Magic in Manhattan series, *Gimme a Call*, and a bunch of other books for teens and tweens, including the Upside-Down Magic series, which she cowrites with Lauren Myracle and Emily Jenkins and which was adapted into a movie for the Disney Channel. Originally from Montreal, Sarah lived in New York City for many years and now lives in Los Angeles with her family. Visit Sarah online at sarahm.com and find her on Instagram at @sarahmlynowski.